IRON POST CORNER

IRON POST CORNER

Clayton Lucas

HAWAII WAY PUBLISHING

HAWAII WAY PUBLISHING
4118 West Harold Ct., Visalia, CA 93291
www.HAWAIIWAYPUBLISHING.com
HAWAII Way logo and name/acronym, Health And Wealth And Inspired Ideas
are registered and trademarked by HAWAII Way Publishing.

HAWAII Way Author/Speakers Agency can send authors to your live
event. For more information or to book Clayton Lucas at an event, contact
HAWAII Way Publishing at: info@HAWAIIWaypublishing.com or by
phone at 559-972-4168

Printed in the United States of America

ISBN 978-1-945384-13-4

DEDICATION

Dedicated to Grandpa and my childhood friend, Heather. You
are missed.

-- As well as all who have ever loved and lost --

ACKNOWLEDGEMENTS

A special thanks to my wife, Lora, for gently encouraging me to follow my dreams. To my children, Clayton III, Jonah, Willie, Henry and Heather for teaching me to cherish the small things and savor each of life's precious moments. To Cindy Lattimore, my 7th grade English teacher, for encouraging me, both in youth and as an adult, to continue writing and to share my work. And, finally, to Season Burch, my amazing agent and publisher, for believing in me and taking the time to answer an unscheduled phone call one afternoon and giving an aspiring writer a few minutes of her crazy busy, yet wonderful life.

PROLOGUE

The young man's name was Tony Charles Arthur Crambrink II. He was the only gringo on a flight from Maracaibo, Venezuela to Willemstad, Curacao, two places most Americans had never even heard of. He had spent the past two years working as a petroleum engineer amongst the hospitality and kindness of the Venezuelan people. He had not planned to return to the states yet but the impending trip was inevitable. He was long overdue for the mandatory safety training that Halliburton required of all engineers every two years. He had put it off for so long that his supervisor finally made the travel arrangements for him. After a short layover in Willemstad, he quickly fell asleep until a flight attendant nudged Tony on the shoulder to wake him.

"Suba el asiento por favor."

1

She was asking him to put his seat forward for landing. As he pushed the button to return his seat to its upright position, he marveled at his relatively new ability to understand and communicate in another language. While other engineers struggled to learn the language -- a requirement of the job -- it seemed to flow naturally for Tony. That was the easy part, he thought to himself. It was the intense heat of a region referred to by the locals as "the land of the beloved sun" that really got to him. However, after the first year, Tony learned to enjoy the extreme temperatures. Living on the shores of beautiful Lake Maracaibo in Cabimas didn't hurt either.

After landing, the flight attendant advised the passengers that they could use their cell phones. Watching everyone simultaneously power up their phones only emphasized Tony's return to life in the fast lane. It made him grateful to live in a country that was at least a decade behind in technology. Email had been his only means of communication with the outside world. Tony embraced the solace that the distance from his family brought him. In fact, since his grandpa didn't have email, Tony had not communicated with any of them since moving to Venezuela. After college, Grandpa Charley had encouraged him to go and it was the best thing he ever did. In fact, he was already anxious to get back. Once off the plane, Tony found a payphone just inside the terminal and made a collect call to his mother.

"Hello."

"Hey, Mom. It's me. I'm back for a few days."

"It's so good to hear from you. How has life been treating you in South America?"

It was good to talk to his mother, he thought. However, by the tone of her voice, it didn't take Tony long to realize that something was wrong.

"Mom, what's wrong?"

"Tony, I know you just got back. It's just that, well, I'm not sure how to tell you…"

"It's OK, Mom. Just tell me what's going on."

"Um, well, I was reading the local obituaries a couple months back and, um, your Grandpa Charley in Sallisaw passed away."

Tony felt a lump form in his throat. His hands went numb, he dropped the receiver and collapsed into the chair next to the payphone. He never imagined feeling such regret for not returning to the farm, for not spending more time with Grandpa Charley. Tony could not understand how it was possible that Grandpa Charley was gone. It was so unexpected. Of course, Grandpa Charley was older, but he was healthy. At least Tony thought he was. Tony realized that he had taken for granted that his grandpa would live forever. The last time they spoke, Grandpa Charley told him that he would see him when he got back. There were so many unanswered questions. How long had Grandpa Charley actually been gone? When was the funeral? Why had no one attempted to contact him through Halliburton? But above all, there was a single question that haunted him more than any other: *Why didn't I return sooner?*

CHAPTER 1

The day finally arrived. Just as with the previous two school years, Heather had waited with great anticipation for this week and it had nothing to do with it being the last week of school. It was the day that she and her seventh grade students would discuss her favorite of all short stories, *"The Lady, or the Tiger"* by Frank Stockton. Heather enjoyed teaching, but writing was her passion. She loved the fact that Stockton purposefully left his tale unfinished, thus relinquishing the fate of his characters into the hands of the reader to determine the valiant triumph or utter demise of the princess and her soul mate. Heather had written several heartfelt endings to the love story over the years, each with its own intuitive glimpse into her life at that time. However, for Heather, the choice given to the princess was an obvious one.

Heather's class read the story aloud the week before and the assignment to have a finished final draft of the ending was due. At her request, the students passed their homework forward and Heather collected it from the front of each row. She then posed a series of questions to the class.

"So, which door did the wicked King's daughter choose for her star-crossed sweetheart? Did she choose life for him, which inevitably meant his marriage to another woman, or death by the vicious tiger, rather than allowing her soul mate to live his life with another woman?"

Heather was delighted as several hands went up. Suddenly, Mr. Wight, the Junior High Principal, opened her classroom door and interrupted.

"Ms. McDuff, you have an emergency phone call in the office from a Mr. Larry Flood."

Heather's hands immediately felt cold and clammy. She walked swiftly out of the classroom in a futile attempt not to alarm her students. Heather knew that if Mr. Flood was calling, it had to be about Grandpa Charley. Mr. Flood was Grandpa Charley's closest friend. However, he would never call her, especially at school, unless something was seriously wrong. By the time Heather ran through the open office door, she felt like her heart was going to leap right out of her chest. She closed the door to Mr.

Wight's office, picked up the receiver and pushed the red flashing button on the old rotary telephone.

"Hello?"

"Hi, Heather. It's Larry. I knew no one else would call you but I know Charley would want you to know."

Heather's voice quivered. "Know what?"

"Charley was rushed to the hospital early this morning."

Heather immediately felt sick to her stomach.

"Is he OK? What happened?"

Mr. Flood explained that Grandpa Charley never returned to the house for breakfast after going out to do the morning chores. Patty, Grandpa Charley's wife, found him lying unconscious in the granary of the barn. Larry wasn't sure how serious his condition was but Heather could tell by the desperation in his voice that it wasn't good.

"Thank you for calling, Mr. Flood. I'm on my way."

"Heather, they ain't gonna let you see him. They're only allowin' family in."

Heather's heart sank.

"Thank you for calling, Mr. Flood."

Heather hung up the phone and opened the door to find Mr. Wight standing at the office counter. Before she could apologize for needing to leave, Mr. Wight told her to go take care of whatever she needed to take care of. Heather rushed through the open office door and then quickly turned back.

"Mr. Wight, my class!"

7

Mr. Wight smiled and waved her on.

"Your class has already been taken care of, Ms. McDuff. Now get out of here."

While speeding toward the hospital, Heather thought of all the good that Grandpa Charley had accomplished in his life. He had touched so many people's lives, including her own. He was the main reason she returned to Oklahoma after completing her graduate studies at the University of Mississippi.

When Heather was nearly ten years old, her daddy died in a tragic accident and her whole world crumbled. Not long after that, Heather's momma met Jerry Strickland and they were married within a few short months. Looking back, Heather knew her momma was scared of the idea of being a single mother and being alone. From the beginning, her momma had insisted that Heather call Jerry "Dad," which she reluctantly agreed to do in an effort to please her momma.

About a year after they were married, Jerry lost his job as a wireline engineer with an offshore oil company. He never really explained what happened, but as a result, they quickly spent all of the money that her daddy had left them. Her daddy had referred to it as "old money," left to him by businesses set up by his great-great-grandparents, which provided dividend payments to the family. However, after marrying Jerry, Heather's momma was no longer eligible to receive the dividend checks from the McDuff family businesses. After the money ran out, Jerry guaranteed them that everything would be OK. A fact that Heather was slow to believe, even at the tender age of 11.

For Heather, the final straw came when Jerry talked her momma into selling their personal property and home at auction. It was an old tobacco plantation situated on the banks of Bayou Fountain in Baton Rouge. The property had been in the McDuff family for seven generations. While Heather understood that seeing the memory of her daddy everywhere was difficult, she did not believe that selling their home or property was the answer. But as a child, she had no say in the matter. All of a sudden, the life that Heather had expected to continue forever was gone in an instant as the auctioneer's gavel fell on the front porch railing.

"Sold! Sold! Sold, to the man in the blue and white pinstriped suit."

What little didn't sell in the auction was loaded into the back of a moving van and they headed to Oklahoma less than a week later. Jerry explained that he owned a place there and could find work in the oil fields where he had begun his career. As they drove down the driveway for the last time, Heather stared at the reflection of her previous life in the rearview mirror. She was bitter about the hand that life had dealt her. She did not speak again until after they arrived in Oklahoma.

Jerry pulled into the driveway and Heather was appalled at what she saw. It was a rundown double-wide trailer situated on a piece of property no bigger than the courtyard of their previous home. Not exactly the kind of living they had been accustomed to in Baton Rouge. Heather unenthusiastically opened the door of the moving van and landed on the gravel driveway below, fully expecting to dislike everything about the place. Almost instantly, a faint, distinct fragrance floating on the breeze caught her attention. It was a sweet aroma that was instantly familiar. Jerry's voice interrupted her thoughts from the other side of the vehicle.

"Y'all smell that honeysuckle? You don't get that livin' in the city."

He was just trying to justify their move but for the first time he didn't have to. He was right. It was the same sweet fragrance that hung on the heavy summer breeze as Heather and her daddy sat rocking on the front porch of their plantation home. Two large honeysuckle vines clung to the brick wall of their courtyard like barnacles to the hull of a ship.

The fragrance, as much as she hated to admit it, seemed to gently rob her of the bitterness she felt. The more she tried to ignore the calming scent, the stronger it became. Heather looked around and located the source of the honeysuckle. It was several large overgrown bushes, covered in apricot colored blossoms running the length of the neighbor's barbed wire fence. The only place the honeysuckle had been manicured was between three fence posts that had enormous catfish heads on them, displayed like trophies.

On the other side of the fence was a huge blackjack oak tree in the middle of the yard, with several large branches that forked upward and outward, supporting a bright red tree house. It was as if the tree house was in the grasp of a giant hand, the gnarled fingers holding it steadily in place. Heather hoped the tree house belonged to a friend. She yearned for someone who could relate to her, someone she could talk to.

Before he died, her daddy told her that at particularly difficult times in his life, he could feel his grandmother guiding him. He also said that if Heather listened close enough, she would also be able to hear her words. Heather never did hear the whisperings of her great-grandmother, but for the first time, she felt as though her daddy was near. Her momma looked over and saw the tears in her daughter's eyes. She dismissed Heather's feelings as anxiety about being in a new place, but it was so much deeper than that. Heather hated to admit it but she almost felt as if she was home. She reluctantly conceded that just maybe she was where she was supposed to be.

Suddenly, out of the corner of her eye, Heather caught the glimpse of a man in overalls walking toward them. Embarrassed, she quickly wiped the tears from her face.

"Hi, y'all. I'm Hank Crambrink from across the street. Let me give you a hand."

After unloading the moving van, Jerry offered their new neighbor a can of his precious Pabst Blue Ribbon out of the ice chest. Heather overheard Hank say that within the next few days his 11-year-old son would be coming to stay for the summer. This only added to her hope that she might soon have a friend to confide in. For the next several days, Heather stared out her bedroom window toward Hank's place and imagined climbing the ladder to the tree house with his son. About a week later, Heather and her momma were unloading groceries in the driveway when they saw an old white pickup drive by with a dog sitting on top of the cab.

"By golly, he must've fallen off the turnip wagon!"

Heather wasn't sure if her momma was referring to the dog or the driver, but she understood what her momma meant. It was crazy for a dog to ride up there while the truck was in motion, especially at those speeds. Right after the old pickup passed by, Hank drove up in his beat up 1978 green Ford truck. Heather and her momma waved and Hank waved back, as they learned was customary in Sequoyah County. Hank parked the truck and got out. To Heather's surprise, a young boy slid out after him, toting an avocado green suitcase that was nearly as big as he was. *He has to be Hank's son*, she thought to herself, although he was shorter than she imagined, with fire engine red hair.

"Can I go meet him, Momma?"

"No, Heather, you'll have to wait 'til tomorrow. They just walked in the door and I'm sure they need some time to get reacquainted."

Heather argued to no avail. As if that wasn't bad enough, her momma then had the audacity to say, "Who knows, Heather? He might not even like you."

Heather stormed off to her room and slammed the door. She refused to consider any possibility that they would not be the best of friends. For the past week she had spent every day imagining the fun they would have, and now, after all the waiting, he had finally arrived and she wasn't even allowed to introduce herself.

The next morning Heather scarfed down breakfast and ran out the door without giving her momma a chance to respond.

"I'm goin' to Hank's!"

She did not want her momma to come up with some excuse again as to why she couldn't go. Heather crossed the road, walked up the porch steps and knocked on the rickety screen door. Hank's wife, Ellen, answered.

"Can Hank's son come out and play?"

Ellen smiled, as she must have realized that Heather did not even know his name.

"You must be Heather."

"Yes, ma'am."

"Tony's dad told me he had met you and your family. Hold on just a minute, sweetie. Tony! You've got a friend here to see you."

"I ain't got no friends here! Who is it?"

He came to the door.

"Hi, Tony. My name's Heather. We just moved in across the street. You want to come out and play?"

"I ain't got time to play. There's chores to be done and Grandpa Charley's waitin'."

Heather immediately remembered the words of her momma and she turned to walk away, feeling frustrated and upset until she was startled by Ellen yelling at Tony.

"Tony!"

13

Heather turned around just in time to see Ellen give Tony that look. Heather knew it all too well. It was the same look that Jerry gave her every time she called him by his given name rather than "Dad." In exactly the same way that Heather always did, Tony relented.

"But you can come with me, even if you are a girl."

Heather stepped back up to the door. Her eyes widened as the excitement quickly grew within her.

"Are you sure it's OK?"

Tony looked back at Ellen, still giving him the look, and then turned back toward Heather.

"I guess so."

Heather wasn't sure what being a girl had to do with anything and she really didn't care. Her summer with her new friend had finally begun. At first, nothing was said. She followed him around the trailer, through a rusty metal gate built out of old pipe and chicken wire, down a well-trodden path toward an old ramshackle barn just north of Hank's trailer. The tin sheets that comprised its roof were completely oxidized and rusted. The planks of wood that made up the walls were weathered and grayed. The closer they got to the barn, the more chickens, ducks, geese and several other fowl instinctively made their way toward them with the expectation of being fed. Heather was admiring a beautiful peacock fanning its tail feathers out, which blocked its view from behind, when Tony snuck up behind it and grabbed it by the tail feathers. The peacock began hollering and flapping its wings in a vain attempt to fly

14

away as all of the other animals scattered. Tony held on tight as the peacock lifted off the ground, rising above his head. The peacock's call continued getting louder while the heavy breeze from the bird's wings beat Heather's hair into her face. Tony finally let go and the peacock landed near a grey soccer-ball-sized bird with a white head that Heather thought looked like a cross between a turkey and a chicken. It flapped its wings and leapt into the air right at Heather. She screamed and jumped backward as Tony began laughing.

"That guinea's more scared of you than you are of it!"

"What's a guinea?"

Tony was now laughing so hysterically that Heather could barely make out what he said.

"Ain't you ever heard of a guinea?"

Embarrassed and quickly trying to change the subject Heather asked, "So why'd you grab that peacock, anyway?"

"'Cause that's what cowboys do. We wrangle stuff."

They continued past the barn toward a large garden and a modest brick home. In the driveway was the same white truck that had passed by the day before with the dog on top of the cab. Heather explained what she had seen and Tony told her that Sarge liked riding on top of the cab of Grandpa Charley's truck. Heather ran her fingers along the side of the truck just before they walked into the backyard. A hedge of bushes outlined the yard with a large catalpa tree just off center. A tire swing hung from the tree's largest

15

branch. Heather grabbed the rope that was tied to the old tire and looked at Tony.

"You want to take turns swinging?"

"We ain't got time to swing. I told you, there's chores to be done."

Just then, they were startled by a voice.

"Now, Tony, there's always time for a little swingin'. Besides, from the sound of it, you already started in on the peacocks."

They hadn't noticed Tony's grandpa standing on the back porch. He was a tall, thin man sporting a grey Stetson with his belt buckle fastened toward the left side of his waist and the face of his watch on the underside of his wrist.

"Who do you have there with you, Number Two?"

At the time, Heather wondered why he referred to Tony as "Number Two."

Tony answered, "That's Heather. Her family just moved in across the street. Ellen made me bring her and she's a girl."

Grandpa Charley laughed.

"Well, howdy there, Heather. It's a pleasure to make your acquaintance. I'm Grandpa Charley."

Grandpa Charley was surprised that Tony had a friend tagging along, especially a girl friend, but it all made sense after Tony explained that Ellen was involved. She just wanted him out of the house so she could watch her soap operas uninterrupted. This delighted Grandpa Charley because each day, as soon as Ellen conned Tony into going outside, he headed straight for Grandpa Charley's house. Grandpa Charley looked at Heather and smiled.

"We would be delighted to have you join us, that is, if you're not afraid of a little farm work."

"No, sir. I take the trash out and do the dishes at my house every day."

"Well then, I'm sure you'll do just fine."

Grandpa Charley scooped Heather up, sat her in the swing and propelled her high into the air. Heather screamed with joy as she swung back and forth. She felt her stomach approach her throat with each rise and fall of the horizon. After Heather came to a stop, Grandpa Charley picked Tony up, set him in the swing and pushed the swing, running all the way underneath before letting go. Tony grinned from ear to ear as the breeze messed up his neatly parted red hair. Afterward, they continued to the barn's granary where Grandpa Charley showed them the different bins of feed for each type of animal before allowing them to fill their coffee cans with chicken scratch.

Later that night, Tony and Grandpa Charley sat in front of the TV watching the mini-series Lonesome Dove while eating cheese, bologna and crackers. Their midnight snack, as they referred to it. Grandpa Charley briefly teased Tony about having a girlfriend and Tony became agitated.

"I ain't got no girlfriend, Grandpa Charley. I told you, the only reason I brought her along was because Ellen made me."

Grandpa Charley laughed.

"Well, then I guess you better bring her back tomorrow so Ellen doesn't blow a cork."

Tony agreed. Although Grandpa Charley knew that he had given Tony the excuse he was looking for to bring Heather back.

From that first meeting, Grandpa Charley knew there was something special about Heather. He felt that Tony knew it too, even if his 11-year-old pride wouldn't allow him to admit it. That was the first of many days they spent together for the next three summers and every other weekend in between. That experience provided Heather a glimpse into the special bond shared between a grandchild and a grandparent. She never had the privilege of knowing her own grandparents but Grandpa Charley was exactly how she imagined them.

Those were happy times, until Hank divorced Ellen, remarried and, as far as Grandpa Charley was concerned, ruined all of their lives.

CHAPTER 2

She was known throughout the county as a homewrecker and, after what happened, Grandpa Charley believed that her name never merited mentioning. The majority of her previous relationships had been with married men. Hank was no different. Regrettably, it took Grandpa Charley some time before he realized how dire the situation was. "That woman," as Grandpa Charley so despisingly referred to her, had been with Hank several times while he was married to Ellen.

Ellen was a local schoolteacher and she arrived home every day at 4:00 p.m., which obviously Hank was aware of. After the first time she came home from work and caught the two of them in her bed together, she forgave Hank. However, the second time that it happened less than a month later, Ellen finally gave in to what Hank wanted all along and moved out. He was more inclined to run Ellen off by breaking her poor heart than to do the right thing and tell her that it was over. Grandpa Charley was greatly troubled by the thought of who his son had become. *I certainly didn't raise him that way*, Grandpa Charley told himself. Years earlier, Hank had done the same thing to Tony's mother when he cheated on her with Ellen. As far as Grandpa Charley was concerned, that should have been Ellen's first clue. If Hank was willing to cheat with her, then Grandpa Charley believed that Ellen should have expected him to cheat on her. But then again, Grandpa Charley always said that if Ellen's brains had been leather, she wouldn't have had enough to saddle a June bug.

After Ellen moved out, Hank's girlfriend and her two small children moved in. However, within a week, a county judge gave custody of her children to their father due to allegations of child endangerment from one of her previous patrons, who just happened to be a relative of the local sheriff. Grandpa Charley tried to protect Tony as much as possible but despite his best efforts, Tony was aware of everything going on. Tony told Grandpa Charley that he understood why Ellen left, but he just couldn't believe that she left without so much as a goodbye after acting as if she cared about him all those years.

Near the end of July, Hank told Grandpa Charley, in front of Tony, that he had full intentions of marrying that woman. Grandpa Charley told him that she would bring him nothing but misery and betrayal just as she had so many others before him. But as usual, Hank believed that he knew better. Shortly after that, Tony went to Grandpa Charley crying.

"Grandpa Charley, I'm scared."

Grandpa Charley knew that he was going through a lot. He dropped to a knee and put his arms around Tony.

"What happened, son?"

"I overheard Dad's girlfriend tell him that she wasn't going to marry him unless he sent me back to my mom's for good."

"Tony, surely you misunderstood. Why would she say that?"

"She told him that it wasn't fair for Dad to have me there if she couldn't have her own kids there."

"Now listen here, my boy. Your dad may be a lot of things but there is no way that he would ever choose that woman over you. If she forces that on him, she'll be gone. And, no matter what, you always have a place here." To his utter disbelief, Grandpa Charley could not have been more wrong about Hank. Grandpa Charley never even got to say goodbye to Tony. By the time Grandpa Charley found out what had happened, it was too late.

Heather was in Tony's front yard when they loaded his suitcase into the truck. He was visibly upset. As they drove away, Tony waved until Heather could no longer see him. When Hank and the woman returned, the words "Just Married" were written in the back window of the truck. Heather went and told Grandpa Charley what she had seen and he immediately confronted Hank.

"Tell me something, Hank, how could a father choose a selfish, inconsiderate, immoral woman over his own son?"

Hank justified his actions by quoting the bible in a twisted and warped way:

"'Therefore shall a man leave his father and his mother, and shall cleave unto his wife and they shall be one flesh.' It doesn't say anything about cleaving unto one's children, and I have every intention of obeying God's commandment to cleave unto my wife."

Grandpa Charley raised his voice in anger.

"Just like you cleaved to Ellen? Just like you cleaved to Tony's mother? Hank, you're a fool if you believe that."

"Despite what you think, old man, I will save her from her previous life."

"You're nothing but a coward and a hypocrite that refuses to stand up for what you know is right. You don't deserve to carry the Crambrink name and you sure don't deserve Tony!"

"Get out of my house and off of my property, old man!"

While it was technically Grandpa Charley's property that he had always allowed Hank to live on, Grandpa Charley walked away and they never spoke again. As far as Grandpa Charley was concerned, there was nothing Hank could ever do to right the wrong he did to that little boy. Grandpa Charley could never forgive Hank. After several weeks of failed attempts to speak with Tony over the phone, Grandpa Charley drove to Tony's mother's house. She refused to let him see Tony. She was furious with the entire family. Grandpa Charley didn't blame her. Just like Ellen, she had also been devastated by Hank, and now he had done the same thing to their son. To make matters worse, Grandpa Charley felt like he had lied to Tony about how his father would react to that woman's ultimatum. This caused him to feel personally responsible for the deep hurt felt by Tony and his mother, even though it was completely out of his control. Grandpa Charley had promised Tony that he would always be there for him and, in the end, he wasn't. He had few regrets in life but now there were two that were lodged in the recesses of his soul. After his first regret, Grandpa Charley promised himself that he would never let anyone get that close again. Little did he know that he would be defenseless against a little redheaded boy and his childhood friend.

CHAPTER 3

Grandpa Charley woke up in the hospital not knowing how he got there or why. Machines chimed all around him. He counted 14 tubes and wires coming out of every place imaginable. His first inclination was to rip them out and walk right out the front door. However, he figured it better to wait and find out what was wrong before doing anything drastic. The last thing he remembered was being in the barn. He had just filled two coffee cans with oats for Boomer and Big Boy, his horses. Next thing he knew, he was in the hospital. Just outside the partially open sliding glass door, Grandpa Charley could hear Patty talking to someone. However, a large curtain obstructed his view.

"For the moment, his condition is stable but we will not know the extent of the damage until the test results are back from the lab. Because we do not have a lab on-site, we had to send his blood work and tissue samples to Fort Smith. It will be anywhere from 24 to 48 hours before we have the results back but I can tell you that his condition is serious."

"Aren't you the least bit concerned about waiting that long? What if he has another episode?"

"Mrs. Crambrink, if I thought transferring your husband was in his best interest, I assure you, I would do that. But with his condition stabilized, there's nothing more any other hospital could do for him than what we are already doing. I'll let you know as soon as I know more."

Grandpa Charley then heard Cindy, their granddaughter, ask Patty if she could move in with her. Patty told her that she was dividing all of the property, including the house, between their two sons, Hank and Cindy's father, Dave, and she would have to ask their permission. *No doubt they are all just waiting on me to buy the farm so they can have mine, he thought.* As far as Grandpa Charley was concerned, they could have it. It comforted him to know that they would all be so caught up bickering over what little they thought he had that they would never learn of his real assets. There were only two other people aware of what he had planned and there was no way they were talking. One of them was bound by attorney/client privilege and Grandpa Charley trusted the other

25

person to the ends of the earth. As for his condition, he was tired and a little sore, but overall he felt OK.

Grandpa Charley had never been seriously ill a day in his life, yet there he was, laid up in the hospital. Probably the one place on earth he felt the least comfortable. That is, except for church. Grandpa Charley had believed in God for as long as he could remember. However, life had taught him that sometime, somewhere, a man had to answer for the wicked that he'd done. And Grandpa Charley had done things that, in his mind, were irreparable. Those things forever changed the course of not only his life but the lives of those dearest to him. Grandpa Charley knew his time was coming sooner than later. He thought it ironic how the reality of old age and being in his current predicament could sober up a heart, even one as stubborn and strong willed as his. He had known for some time what he needed to do but he had been slow to act. He worried about causing Tony more heartache. However, Grandpa Charley had learned the hard way that if Tony didn't confront his past, he would eventually have regrets similar to those of Grandpa Charley and he was unwilling to allow Tony to feel that kind of pain. Grandpa Charley finally concluded that it was time to do everything within his power to right his wrongs or regret them forever.

In the past, Grandpa Charley had been unsure how to carry out his plan. Due to Tony's relationship with his dad, or lack thereof, he was slow to trust. Grandpa Charley needed to find someone that had forged a strong bond with Tony long before all of the hurt took place. Then, when Heather moved back to town, it all became obvious to Grandpa Charley. Heather was the only one that had any chance of getting through to Tony, even if she didn't know it.

Now, lying in the hospital, Grandpa Charley had to figure out how to contact her. He knew she would be in class until the afternoon but afterward he planned to sneak a call to her. Grandpa Charley quietly snickered, content with his usual sneaky self.

Heather arrived at the hospital. The parking lot closest to the Emergency Room was full and the only space available was marked "Clergy Parking." Heather didn't care. She parked and ran inside into a waiting room full of people. She impatiently waited in line behind a large woman who was pleading with the nurse at the front desk to move her to the top of the list of waiting patients. The woman was justifying why her condition was so much worse than everyone else's. Heather's thoughts turned back to Grandpa Charley and she wondered if she had arrived in time. She immediately dismissed any such thought. Heather questioned whether he really knew how important he was to her. In her heart, she prayed for the chance to tell him at least one more time, but feared that Patty would deny her the opportunity as she had tried to do so many times in the past. Grandpa Charley's family had never accepted her because she was not blood, not a true Crambrink, as Patty liked to remind her.

Snapping Heather out of her trance-like state, the nurse called the woman in front of her by name and abruptly told her that she would have to wait her turn just like everyone else. The woman became very agitated and began yelling. "I'm in pain! I need my pills and y'all are refusin' my treatment!"

She had everyone in the Emergency Room's attention as she stomped out of the main entrance, raving, "I'm fixin' to write a letter to the Sequoyah County Times! This ain't right!"

The nurse turned her attention to Heather, speaking politely, "Sorry about that, dear. She's a regular. Can I help you?"

"Yes, ma'am. I'm looking for Charley Crambrink."

With a few quick strokes of her keyboard, the nurse explained that he was still in the E.R. Heather felt a strong sense of peace flow through her. *He's still with me,* she thought to herself.

"Are you Mr. Crambrink's kin?"

"Yes, ma'am. I'm his granddaughter."

"Bless your heart. Go on in. He's in Room 118."

The nurse pushed a button underneath the desk and two large automatic doors opened. Heather rushed in and began searching for Grandpa Charley's room. At last, there it was. She slowly walked in through the open sliding door and waited just behind the curtain while a nurse finished checking on Grandpa Charley. The nurse moved out of the way just enough for Heather to see his face. She winked at him and he smiled back at her. He didn't give a second thought to how she found out. He knew his buddy, Larry, had his back.

As the nurse finished up and left the room, Heather rushed to his side, laid her head on his chest and whispered, "I love you, Grandpa Charley."

28

Heather was so in the moment and focused on Grandpa Charley that she failed to see Patty and Cindy sitting between the end of the bed and the curtain she had been standing behind. Had she noticed them, she certainly would have taken a more subtle approach.

Cindy jumped out of her chair and started shouting, "What in the heck is she doin' here? She ain't family!"

Cindy had always been jealous of the relationship that Grandpa Charley and Heather shared. However, with Patty, it was different. It wasn't personal. Heather was not family, plain and simple. The nurse overheard the yelling and quickly ran back in the room, looking at Heather:

"I'm sorry, sweetie, but if you're not family, you can't be in here."

Heather could not believe that, in his greatest time of need, Grandpa Charley's family refused to put their selfishness aside long enough to help him through this. She felt her eyes begin to burn as the tears welled up. Heather wanted to tell Cindy and Patty where to go but she knew it wouldn't do any good and it definitely would not help Grandpa Charley. Heather put her hand on his chest and gave him a wink.

"I'll see you soon."

Heather quickly turned around to keep Grandpa Charley from seeing her tears and walked out the door.

Grandpa Charley sat up in his bed and the nurse shoved him back down as he began yelling, "Now wait just a dad gum minute! That one's off her rocker!"

He then turned his focus toward Heather. "That's my granddaughter and if she ain't family neither are they!"

During the commotion, Grandpa Charley's IV was caught on the bed rail and ripped from his hand. Blood ran down his arm and onto the bed sheets. Now the nurse was also yelling, "I need some help in here! All of y'all get out now!"

Two more nurses rushed in to hold Grandpa Charley down. Heather was frustrated but at least she knew that Grandpa Charley was well enough to sit up in bed and shout at the top of his lungs. She was also elated to hear him stand up for her when he told them that she was as much family as they were. His words had angered them and Heather was glad. Most of the time she tolerated them out of respect for Grandpa Charley but today was different. She wasn't going to allow the sharpness of their words to cut through those few precious seconds she had with him. Heather turned and waved to him one last time before walking out of sight. The last thing she saw was Grandpa Charley finally relenting to the three nurses holding him down.

As she approached the nurse's station, she could still hear Grandpa Charley. "Y'all don't know who you're dealin' with. I'm Tony Charles Arthur Crambrink and you either get my granddaughter back in here or you'll be pushin' daisies by mornin'."

Heather couldn't help but smile. She was moved by Grandpa Charley's passion, especially because it was directed at her.

Upset did not begin to explain how Grandpa Charley felt as Heather was forced from his room. He was surprised that the nurses did not heed his commands. He was known throughout Sequoyah County and was as influential as anyone. He couldn't believe that one of the nurses even had the audacity to mock him. "I know exactly who you are, Tony Charles Arthur Crambrink and if you'll calm down and listen, you'll get exactly what's comin' to you."

She obviously doesn't know who she's dealing with, Grandpa Charley thought to himself. His attorney was the president of the hospital board and he had full intentions of making sure this crazy nurse never worked in Sallisaw again. Still, he was grateful for the opportunity to see Heather. When she walked out of the room, Grandpa Charley noticed the tears in her eyes, even though she attempted to conceal them. There wasn't much she could hide from her grandpa, he thought.

Heather walked to the nurse's station and asked the supervising nurse what Grandpa Charley's status was. The nurse reviewed his chart and turned to the second page.

"It looks like he's stable at the moment but he'll be admitted until…"

Patty interrupted, "She ain't kin. Don't you dare tell her nothin' else."

The nurse looked at Heather regretfully.

31

"I'm sorry, honey, but she's right. We're only allowed to discuss a patient's condition with members of the immediate family."

Cindy snickered, making no attempt to conceal her amusement, which further infuriated Heather. They had no genuine concern for anyone but themselves. Patty turned toward Heather.

"Heather, just like I been tellin' you for years. Blood is thicker than water and, in the end, he'll choose us over you. You aren't the first woman to believe you could come between us."

Heather walked away, defeated. She did not want to believe Patty's words but Heather knew that she was right. They were, indeed, Grandpa Charley's family, related by blood and marriage, and she was not. Heather had never wanted Grandpa Charley to choose her over them. Nor did she have any desire to come between them. She just wanted to feel like she belonged, to be part of Grandpa Charley's life. He always had a way of making her feel wanted and special. Heather walked out of the hospital, hurt and disappointed.

As she replayed Patty's words in her mind, she wondered who had attempted to come between them in the past. As Heather arrived at her vehicle, Patty and Cindy slowly drove by in Grandpa Charley's truck. Wearing Grandpa Charley's grey Stetson, Cindy sneered through the window. "Look, Grandma! She's in the preacher parkin'. Think you can save Grandpa Charley, preacher lady?"

32

That southern flare was alive and well inside Heather. It was all she could do to refrain from giving Cindy the one fingered salute. However, being a McDuff from Baton Rouge, she was above such barbaric gestures. Heather opened the door of her car and collapsed into the front seat, feeling overwhelmed. She closed the door and started the car. Suddenly, she was startled by someone frantically knocking on her window. When she saw that it was Grandpa Charley's nurse, Heather was concerned until she realized that the nurse was smiling. Heather turned off the car and stepped back out. The nurse was completely out of breath. She put one hand on Heather's shoulder and the other on her hip as she took several seconds to catch her breath. To Heather's amazement, the nurse told her that she could return to Grandpa Charley's room now that Patty and Cindy were gone. Heather was grateful but confused. She asked why the nurse was allowing her back in to see Grandpa Charley, especially knowing that she wasn't really related to him.

"I know what family is and what it ain't. Those other two that got there before you ain't what I'd call family. I don't care who they're related to. Besides, I'd give that man my right arm if he asked for it. He don't recognize me but my maiden name is Flood. My uncle Larry owns the feed store where your Grandpa Charley buys feed."

Heather instantly knew that she was Mr. Flood's niece, Julie. As kids, Heather and Tony occasionally accompanied Grandpa Charley to the feed store and it was not unusual for Julie to be there.

Julie continued, "I don't know the whole story, but before I was born, my uncle Larry's house was being repossessed by the bank and they were in danger of losing everything, including the store. Somehow, your grandpa saved them from foreclosure. Uncle Larry never would tell us the whole story. All he would say is, remember Mr. Crambrink in your prayers. There were always rumors that your grandpa paid off the bank with some stolen fortune he dug up, but you know how rumors are."

They both laughed knowing that while Grandpa Charley had done OK for himself, he was not a rich man by any stretch of the imagination. Grandpa Charley worked for everything he had and his only means of income came from his Army pension and his small cattle operation. Heather had never heard that story, but Grandpa Charley's generosity did not surprise her. It now made sense why Mr. Flood and Grandpa Charley were the best of friends.

"Heather, it was a pleasure to see you again, but I had better get you back in there before I'm listed as missing on the front page of the newspaper."

They laughed again. Heather thanked Julie before they parted ways in front of Grandpa Charley's room. Heather gently slid the door open, thinking she would surprise him. However, when she walked past the curtain, he was grinning at her, almost beaming, as if he had planned the whole thing.

"Hey there, Grandpa Charley. Me being back in here wouldn't have anything to do with you threatening some defenseless nurse, would it?"

"Why do you ask? Did she say somethin'?"

"She might have mentioned a concern about ending up on the front page of the Sequoyah County Times."

Grandpa Charley laughed as Heather's comments confirmed that he had gotten under the nurse's skin.

"As long as she continues to go with the program, she's got nothin' to worry about."

"Grandpa Charley, that nurse isn't as crazy as you think she is. If you only knew."

Grandpa Charley seemed puzzled by the insight Heather gained in the short time since leaving his room. Heather was proud to have gotten one up on Grandpa Charley, especially because that rarely happened.

"How are you feeling?"

"You know there ain't nothin' that could keep old Number One down."

His reference to "Number One" reminded her of Tony. Heather realized that she thought of Tony more often than she liked to admit. She was still so angry with him for not staying in touch with Grandpa Charley. Of all people, she understood what he had gone through as a kid because she had been there too. It had been difficult on all of them.

"Speaking of Tony, have you heard from him lately?"

Heather immediately regretted her question. Grandpa Charley was surprised and delighted. It was the first time in a long time that Heather started a conversation about Tony.

35

"I haven't heard from him since right before you moved back to Sallisaw. I know we haven't talked about him much but hear me out. At least let me explain why he left for South America."

Grandpa Charley told her that Tony had called shortly before graduating from Penn State in Petroleum Engineering. He was grateful for the money Grandpa Charley had given him to pay for his education. Tony always made it a point to thank him when they talked but Grandpa Charley felt like it was the least he could do. Tony was looking for work and wanted to move back to Oklahoma to work in the oil industry and be closer to the farm. However, the only job he had been offered was with the Halliburton Company, which would require him to move overseas.

"Tony, are you not interested in the job with Halliburton?"

"Well, yeah. I think experiencing life in another country would be exciting, but then who knows when I would be able to visit?"

"Tony, how much more will you make with Halliburton than you would make with an oil company in Oklahoma?"

"With gas prices being what they are, stateside petroleum engineering jobs are few and far between. Even if I could find one, it would probably pay less than half of what I would make with Halliburton in Venezuela. But it's not about the money, Grandpa Charley."

"Number Two, you have a great trip. I'll send you a check, my boy."

Grandpa Charley always sent Tony a check. It was his way of telling Tony that he loved him without saying the words. He didn't have to say them. Tony had always known since he was a little boy. Not to mention that without Grandpa Charley's financial assistance, Tony would never have been able to attend college.

"But, Grandpa Charley, I haven't really spent any time with you since I was a kid and I'd like to help you out on the farm like I used to."

"Now listen here, Number Two. These jobs don't just come around every day. You have to take advantage of an opportunity when it comes along. That's how I was promoted to Master Sergeant in the Army at such a young age. I was willing to go where no one else wanted to go and do what no one else was willing to do. It's what took me to California, and Lord knows I wouldn't be who I am had I never gone to California. But that's a story for another day. You are a Crambrink. Don't make the same mistake I did, son. Follow your dreams."

Grandpa Charley always ended their conversations the same way. "Old Number One will be waitin' on Number Two. I'll see you when you get back."

Grandpa Charley finished his story and looked at Heather.

"Heather, I told him to take that job and move to Valenzuela."

Heather thought it was sweet how Grandpa Charley mispronounced the country's name. It made her smile, which helped her hide her true feelings regarding Tony. As much as Heather loved Grandpa Charley, she felt that he always made excuses for Tony.

"Heather, Tony is still trying to find himself, but when the time is right, he will return."

Heather had the sudden, unintentional thought, *"Whatever!"*

She believed Grandpa Charley had a better chance of getting oil from a waterspout than getting Tony to come back to Oklahoma. When she was younger, she believed Tony to be better than that. She believed him to be more like Grandpa Charley, but as the years went by, she determined that he was just like the rest of the Crambrinks.

"Heather, I hope you give Tony a chance when he comes back. You just might find the friend you once knew."

Heather wondered if Grandpa Charley had intuitively read her thoughts. She hoped not because she knew that he would be hurt if he were aware that she didn't believe him. Heather was a realist and life had taught her that people change and move on with their lives. That was most certainly the case with Tony, she thought. He had moved on with his life and left the two of them behind without any thought or regard for their feelings. Heather convinced herself that she didn't care what Tony thought of her, but it made her sad that Tony didn't care enough to ever visit Grandpa Charley.

Grandpa Charley could tell that Heather was irritated. He admired her tenacity and flare. As far as he was concerned, Heather was every bit the sassy southern belle that her daddy would have been so very proud of. Grandpa Charley had always been honored to call her his granddaughter.

All of a sudden, Grandpa Charley's expression changed. He became very serious and told Heather that he had some very important things to say to her. At first, she told him that they had all summer and as soon as he was home from the hospital, they could discuss whatever he wanted. At that moment, Grandpa Charley's eyes conveyed a sense of urgency that she had never before sensed from him.

"Heather, my dear, I love you. It's time you knew who I really am and where I came from. It's a story that I need you to share with Tony. He needs to have a better understanding of his own past, which will help him understand why things are the way they are. I believe you are the only one that can get through to him."

Heather sat and listened to Grandpa Charley into the early morning hours. Their only interruptions came from the nurses checking on him. That night Heather promised him that, if given the opportunity, she would share his story with Tony the next time she saw him. Grandpa Charley told her that she needed to heed her thoughts, impressions and feelings, no matter how difficult, when Tony came back. She really didn't understand what he meant until he told her to "follow the breadcrumbs." It had become their slogan. It was Grandpa Charley's way of telling Heather to seek out her own destiny while paying attention to opportunities along the way. Grandpa Charley made it obvious that night that he believed that Tony coming back to Oklahoma was one of those opportunities.

"Heather, you once told me that the sweet smell of honeysuckle instantly changed your perspective about moving to Sallisaw and, in that moment, you knew that you were where you belonged. Look at how that perspective changed your life. In the same way, there will be other things that will speak to your heart if you listen."

Tears streamed down Heather's face. His words reminded her of things her daddy had shared with her as a young girl.

"Grandpa Charley, I'll do anything you ask, just promise me that you'll always be with me."

Grandpa Charley's reply pierced the center of her heart.

"My dear Heather, this old confederate is 89 years young and no matter what the doctors say is or ain't wrong with me, my time on this old earth is limited."

Grandpa Charley had a way with words. Grandpa Charley's careful selection and use of the word confederate was a reference to his father. During the handful of times that his father visited, he referred to Grandpa Charley as his "little confederate," meaning that they were allies banded together through life's circumstances. Back then, Grandpa Charley had no idea the man was his father. The last time they saw each other, Grandpa Charley was eight years old. It was one of the few things Heather knew about his past. However, that night she learned why Grandpa Charley rarely talked about his past, and it broke her heart. Yet the truth of the matter was, Heather still didn't know the half of it.

CHAPTER 4

It had been more than a month since Grandpa Charley's passing. Visiting Grandpa Charley at the cemetery quickly became Heather's safe haven when she was feeling lonely or just needed someone to talk to. Death had not hindered Grandpa Charley's ability to listen. Almost daily, Heather replaced the flowers in a permanent concrete vase next to his tombstone and sat down to discuss with him, as if he were present, whatever was on her mind. Although she almost always ended up talking about the details of their last conversation that night in the hospital.

Of everything Grandpa Charley told her, there was one thing that seemed to stand out above all else. "Sweetheart, if you promise to visit me at the cemetery after I'm gone, you'll eventually find what you're lookin' for."

Grandpa Charley then laughed.

"Besides, I'll need the company."

At the time, Heather didn't see anything funny about it. She wondered how Grandpa Charley seemed to know just what she was looking for in life when she had no clue. Heather missed him so much. Each time she drove away from the cemetery she passed Flood's Feed Store. It reminded her of the priceless gift that Grandpa Charley's nurse had given them the day before Grandpa Charley's passing. He had told Heather that his time on earth was short, although neither of them had any idea how prophetic those words would be.

Grandpa Charley fell asleep late that night after they finished their conversation. Heather never left his side. Sitting in the chair next to his hospital bed, she fell asleep sometime after he did and she awoke to a steady alarm. It was Grandpa Charley's heart monitor. Nurses rushed in but it was too late. He was gone. They disconnected him from the monitors and made no attempt to revive him.

"Aren't you going to perform CPR?"

"I'm sorry, sweetie, but he had a DNR on file. There's nothing more we can do."

Unbeknownst to anyone, Grandpa Charley had filed a "Do Not Resuscitate" letter with the hospital several years before. He never wanted to live a life where others had to take care of him. Heather was devastated, and while she respected his wishes, she didn't think it was fair. She was, however, grateful for those last precious hours with him before he passed away peacefully in his sleep. The last thing he asked of her was that she pick up a letter from his attorney. Yet everything happened so unexpectedly that it was all just too much for Heather to take in at once. She knew it was silly, but picking up the letter somehow made Grandpa Charley's death more real. She knew that she would pick up the letter when she was ready. She just wasn't there yet.

Within days of the funeral, Heather received a generic email from the Oklahoma Education Association regarding teaching opportunities around the country. She typically ignored such emails because she enjoyed teaching at Central and being close to Grandpa Charley. However, with Grandpa Charley gone, she was curious as to what positions would still be available, since the majority of teachers, including herself, were already under contract for the coming school year. As expected, the list of open positions was relatively short. Yet one position immediately stood out. It was an Associate Professor of Creative Writing at Louisiana State University. At first, Heather was reluctant to apply. She felt guilty about moving away from the farm and away from her visits to the cemetery, not to mention she was already obligated to teach another year at Central. However, not only was the position in her hometown of Baton Rouge, but it was her dream job. She was deeply conflicted until she remembered the words of Grandpa Charley, "Follow the breadcrumbs."

She decided to heed his advice and apply for the job. She wholeheartedly believed that she was following the breadcrumbs. *Besides*, she rationalized, *it's not like they're going to offer me the job, because I don't meet the minimum requirements.* The job announcement stated that at least two years of college level teaching experience were required. Heather had none. She updated her resume and scanned a copy of her credentials anyway. Listed among the other requested application materials was a writing sample. That night Heather authored a new draft of her very personal ending to *The Lady, or the Tiger*. She thought about sending a previous draft but she knew that if she was to have any chance of getting the job, this had to be her finest work ever. And, while she had always required it of her students, this would be the first time that Heather had shared her ending to *The Lady, or the Tiger* with anyone.

After interviewing her twice over the phone, the Department Chair asked Heather to travel to Baton Rouge to interview in person. She told Heather that the selection committee had narrowed the candidates down to her and one other. Heather was shocked to have made the final cut. She flew to Baton Rouge for the first time since leaving there as a child and met with the Department Chair and other tenured professors of the Creative Writing Department. They asked her several questions, though not as many as she had expected. The questions ranged in topic from her teaching style and her lack of experience at the collegiate level to specific questions regarding her writing sample and where her creativity came from. Heather's only concern was that the interview only lasted half an hour. She wondered how they could make an informed decision in such a short period of time.

After the interview, Heather decided to visit her family plantation. The last time she saw it was through the rearview mirror of a moving van when she was 11 years old. On the way, she told herself that she had done all she could to get the job and that it was no longer in her hands. However, Heather knew that she would be extremely disappointed if she were not selected, especially after making it so far in the process. She hoped that walking through the memories at her family property might help her sort out her thoughts and calm her nerves, but nothing could have been further from the truth.

Heather turned onto Highland Road and immediately felt sick to her stomach. All thoughts of the interview and the teaching position were immediately replaced by disturbing memories of her daddy's death. They say that time heals all wounds, yet she still felt responsible. It was as fresh on her mind as the day that it happened. As if she had been transported back in time, Heather could see her daddy's silhouette disappear underneath the water. She grabbed her arm as she, again, felt the pain from being slammed against the side of the boat. She cried out and pulled the car over. The day that her daddy died was the worst day of her life -- before or since. Heather never spoke of the events of that day to anyone, not even Grandpa Charley. In fact, she rarely even thought about it. The pain from the guilt was more than she could bear.

45

Heather turned the car around and headed in the opposite direction, not caring where she was headed. Suddenly, her cell phone rang. Shaken from what had just happened, she instinctively answered the ringing phone without looking to see who it was. Heather attempted to answer but nothing came out.

"Hello."

It was the Department Chair from LSU. Heather, again, tried to say something but she was too emotional. She held the phone away from her face, cleared her throat and quickly composed herself.

"Hello. Ms. McDuff. Can you hear me?"

"Yes, Dr. Lattimore. I'm here."

"I can call you back later if you'd like."

Dr. Lattimore wasn't sure what was wrong with Heather but it was obvious that something was amiss.

"No, no. I'm good. I apologize. I had something in my throat. How can I help you?"

"I know that it is unusual to interview twice in one day but are you available to come back for a final interview?"

Heather thought that her interview earlier that day was the final interview but, of course, she was more than willing to do whatever was required.

"Yes, ma'am. I can be there in about ten minutes if that works."

"Perfect. I'll see you then."

Heather was embarrassed that she had been emotional when Dr. Lattimore called. That was the first time in as long as she could remember that she had recalled the vivid events of that day. She didn't want to think about it. She pushed the memories as far from the surface as she could and drove back to LSU. She parked and pulled the car visor down to check her makeup in the mirror. *Thank goodness for waterproof mascara*, she thought. Heather walked back to the Creative Writing Department and was surprised to find Dr. Lattimore alone. She had not been overly nervous earlier but now that it was a one-on-one interview, she felt her stomach tense. She took a deep breath and walked through the door.

"Welcome back, Ms. McDuff. Come on in and have a seat."

Heather sat down.

"Initially, you were passed over because you have never taught at a university. However, after one of the professors read your writing sample, he passed it around to the rest of us and suggested that we reconsider. That is why we invited you here for an interview earlier today. Your unique spin on *"The Lady, or the Tiger"* was exactly the kind of originality and creativity that we are searching for. This set you above and beyond all of the other applicants."

Heather reflected on her ending to the short story. In summary, she wrote:

Just as the King "was a man of such exuberant fancy that when he agreed upon anything, the thing was done," the princess, being the King's daughter, was even more exuberant and irresistible than he. In fact, the princess "Possessed of more power, influence, and force of character than anyone," even surely the King, which is how she came by her knowledge "of the secret of the doors." The princess had no intention of leaving anything within her sphere of influence, especially the fate of her lover, to the decrees of what her father referred to as "an impartial and incorruptible chance." Like her mother before her, the Princess was a woman of action.

Within the "vast amphitheater, with its encircling galleries, its mysterious vaults, and its unseen passages," the princess secretly commissioned the hollowing out of a new tunnel. It was just large enough for the maiden and the pile of gold offered her to escape the outer walls of the coliseum. The secret tunnel was accessible only through a hidden iron supported door located inside the dark room, and its whereabouts were known only to its maker, the princess, and the young maiden. After being placed inside, the maiden located the secret door, revealing her bounty, and crawled to the outer wall, dragging the bag of gold behind her. Meanwhile, after signaling her lover inside the arena with a signal that only they would recognize or understand, the princess exclaimed, 'I can't watch this!'

The wicked king grinned, amused with himself and his perfect system of chance. The princess left her seat and ran as fast as she could to the nearest exit, where a horse and chariot awaited her. As instructed, the driver raced to the other side of the coliseum, where the princess sprinted to the inner door of the room, all the while hoping she would get there in time. Otherwise, all of her efforts would have been for naught. The door was opened and the princess had successfully taken the place of the young maiden that was originally chosen to share her lover's fate. The angry King stood

48

from his throne and looked down upon his daughter kissing the young man, as the crowd cheered in amazement.

In her infinite wisdom, the princess understood that there were only two possible outcomes: The King could nullify the results, based on the princess' prior knowledge of which door the tiger was in, thereby admitting that his perfect system was flawed; or the King could support the system that he created and sold to the people as "impartial and incorruptible." However, he would lose his daughter to the marriage of her soul mate. Knowing her father the way she did, the princess knew that the King's pride would never allow him to compromise the validity of a system that he, himself, created whose perfect fairness was obvious.

After the princess and her lover embraced, the planned wedding ensued. Eventually, the public became aware of the mercy provided the young maiden by the princess, despite being hated by her. This simple act of kindness gave the princess credibility with her loving people during her long reign after the King's death. The princess and the new prince lived happily ever after.

Every time Heather wrote this story, she saw herself as the princess. When her daddy died, she found herself thrown into a world in which she had no control. However, after moving to Sallisaw, Grandpa Charley had taught her that life was too short to leave to chance. On more than one occasion, he had told her to follow the breadcrumbs of opportunity, while retaining within herself her own fate, just as the princess in the story. That is exactly why she applied for the position at LSU, despite not meeting the minimum requirements. *Grandpa Charley was right,* she thought to herself. She was now a finalist for her dream job because she took a chance and ignored the part she didn't qualify for, which had led her to this meeting with Dr. Lattimore.

Heather could hardly believe the words she heard next. "Ms. McDuff, we would like to offer you a probationary appointment for the first year. It would require you to be here at least one week before the first day of school in September. After the first year, you will be evaluated and considered for a permanent tenured position."

"Thank you so much, Dr. Lattimore. I am honored. I just need to get home and make sure that I can get out of the contract that I signed for the upcoming school year."

"You do realize that if you do not fulfill a local public school contract, that just keeps you from being able to teach at another local public school for that year. It has nothing to do with teaching at a university."

"Yes, ma'am. I understand. But by signing the contract, I made a promise to fulfill my end of the bargain. They have been good to me and I owe them the courtesy of requesting to withdraw."

"I understand. Please call me as soon as you have made your final decision." Heather's loyalty only confirmed to Dr. Lattimore that she was the right person for the job.

Heather couldn't wait to get back to Oklahoma and discuss things with Mr. Wight. After arriving at the airport, Heather drove directly to Central. Mr. Wight told her that she was invaluable to the children of the district and asked her to take at least a week to reconsider. At the end of that week, if she believed it was in her best interest to leave, Mr. Wight said that he would not hold her to the contract. Out of respect for him, Heather agreed to think it over, but she knew there was nothing to reconsider. With Grandpa Charley gone, she needed to move on with her life.

After speaking with Mr. Wight, Heather decided to go see Grandpa Charley's attorney. She not only felt ready to pick up the letter, she was actually at peace with it. She arrived downtown and parked in front of the courthouse. Fitting, she thought, that it was a beautiful sunny day. Her mood was better than it had been since Grandpa Charley's passing. Of course, she still missed him. *I'll always miss him*, she thought. But she felt like things were finally looking up.

Heather walked up to the door of the attorney's office. The scales of justice were embossed on the glass door. Just below the scales was the attorney's name, "W. Clayton Williford." Heather walked through the doors and down the short hallway to the receptionist's desk. The office was dated as wood paneling covered the walls, popcorn texture coated the ceilings and the carpet was faded avocado green.

"May I help you?"

"Yes, ma'am. Is Mr. Williford available?"

"I'm not sure. May I get your name?"

"Heather McDuff. I'm here to pick up a letter from Charley Crambrink."

"Just a minute, dear."

The receptionist left the front office and headed down the back hall. A short time later, she returned with a thin, short man wearing a suit with no tie.

"Hello, Ms. McDuff. I was starting to think you weren't going to stop by."

"About that. Sorry, I just wasn't ready."

"No problem at all. I believe this is what you're looking for."

He handed her a letter-sized white envelope with her name on it. She recognized Grandpa Charley's handwriting.

"I'm sorry for your loss, Ms. McDuff. Mr. Crambrink was an amazing man who did a lot for this community. He will be missed."

She thanked him and turned to leave.

"Excuse me, Ms. McDuff?"

Heather turned back around.

"I have another letter for you but I was instructed to have you give it to Tony when you see him."

Heather laughed.

"Good luck with that. I don't think any of us will ever see him again."

"Charley said that you would say that. However, he believed otherwise. Either way, it was Charley's wish that you deliver this letter to Tony."

"Yeah. Sure thing."

Heather's tone was sarcastic as she took the letter from Mr. Williford. She left the office and headed straight to the cemetery.

52

She hadn't been there in several days due to being in Louisiana and she could not wait to read her letter. However, she wanted to read it with Grandpa Charley present, at least as much as he could be anyway. She parked outside the entrance to the cemetery just as she always did. A number of small roads snaked through the cemetery but Heather enjoyed the walk to Grandpa Charley's plot. She sat down at his tombstone and crossed her legs. She then pulled the letter from her back pocket and waved it back and forth.

"I finally picked up your letter today. Aren't you proud of me? I also have something very important to share with you, but before I do, let's see what was so important that you couldn't tell me in person."

That last night in the hospital, Grandpa Charley made Heather promise to do whatever he asked of her in the letter. She didn't think twice about it. She knew that she would do anything for him. Heather slid her fingernail underneath the flap, ripping it open, and pulled the handwritten letter from the sealed envelope.

"Dearest Heather, if you're reading this, then I have already departed this old earth. I want you to know that you blessed my life and I am proud to call you my granddaughter."

Tears ran down Heather's face. It was as if Grandpa Charley was speaking to her from beyond the grave. She continued reading:

"I could never thank you enough for all of the happiness you brought to my life. You were always there for me when I needed you, whether you realized it or not. That's why asking you to do one last thing for me is so difficult but I know it's necessary."

Heather dropped her hand on her lap while still holding the letter. She smiled and, through misty eyes, looked back at Grandpa Charley's tombstone.

"I told you, Grandpa Charley. I would do anything for you. Name it."

She raised the letter back up and continued reading.

"I know you have hard feelings toward Tony but I need you to find it in your heart to forgive him. I need you to find a way to contact him or wait until he returns to Oklahoma so that the two of you can set things right. You were dear friends once and I know you can be again. Please fulfill the last wish of an old man. It will make your Grandpa Charley's day. Thank you in advance. Love, Grandpa Charley."

By now, Heather's tears had increased. She had gone from grateful just a few minutes prior to deep sadness. She sincerely would have done anything for her beloved Grandpa Charley but the thing he was asking of her was impossible and she knew it.

"Really, Grandpa Charley. I have done everything you have asked and now, after all I have been through, you ask this of me. That important thing I have to tell you. Well, I was offered an amazing job. It would allow me to move back to Baton Rouge and to be a Creative Writing Professor at LSU. Of all people, you know what that means to me."

As much as she tried to ignore them, Heather could feel his words:

"Heather, dear. You promised you would do anything for me. You're right. Above all others, I do understand what that position would mean but you making things right with Tony is just as important. If you'll give it a chance, it will mean a lot to you too. I know you believe in second chances. Be there for him, like you were there for me."

For a split second, Heather thought about what it would mean to stay in Sallisaw. First and foremost, it meant giving up her dream job. It also meant further confrontations with Grandpa Charley's family. Heather could still hear Patty's voice telling her that she wasn't family. Heather plopped her face in her hands and wept. While the tears never ceased, the sadness soon turned to anger. Grandpa Charley had promised her that Tony would return to Sallisaw but he hadn't. Now, with Grandpa Charley gone, she knew that he was far less likely to ever return.

Heather knew that Grandpa Charley really believed in Tony, yet she was nothing but disappointed in him. Out of respect for Grandpa Charley, Heather never shared her thoughts or feelings with him when he was alive, but all of a sudden, it was as if the dam burst: "He's never coming back. Do you hear me? It wouldn't matter if I were able to get hold of him. He didn't care enough to visit you when you were alive. He's not coming back now that you're dead. Grandpa Charley, I'm sorry but I can't do this anymore!"

Heather walked back to her car without turning around like she normally did to wink at Grandpa Charley's tombstone. He was the reason she moved back and now that he was gone, there was nothing to keep her there. She decided that she had been to the cemetery for the last time. She needed to get on with her life and now she had the opportunity to do so. She was going home to make moving arrangements.

CHAPTER 5

Heather drove away from the cemetery, downhearted and discouraged. She reached over and turned on the radio to drown out her thoughts. However, the song by Adele only accentuated them. Heather knew all too well the bitterness and heaviness characterized by Adele's music.

As she started back toward Sallisaw, the vehicle's gas light came on. The only gas station in the area was Flood's Feed Store. Heather had not seen Mr. Flood since the funeral and she wasn't really in the mood to reminisce. However, given her circumstances, she did not have much choice. She parked the car next to the gas pump and walked into the store. Mr. Flood was sitting behind the counter, his glasses on the end of his nose, pen in one hand and a stack of charge accounts in the other. He greeted her without ever looking up and, of course, she said "hi" back. She laid $20 on the counter, hoping that Mr. Flood would not look up and recognize her.

"Twenty on pump number one, please."

Without ever looking up, Mr. Flood laughed. "Heather, we still let people fill up before paying. Besides, your account still has a credit."

Heather must have had a surprised look on her face.

"You didn't think I knew it was you, did you? I may be old, but I still recognize a Crambrink when I see one."

"Mr. Flood, I don't have an account with you and, as much as I wish I were, I'm no Crambrink."

Mr. Flood laid the charge receipts on the counter and took his glasses off.

"Heather, first of all, you will always have an account here and it will always have a credit, so put that $20 back in your purse. Secondly, you're as much a Crambrink as your grandfather was. I'm sincerely sorry for your loss, honey. Your granddad was the best man and best friend I ever knew."

Looking for the words to cut through the awkward silence, Heather attempted to continue the conversation. "Well, I just came from the cemetery." Attempting to keep the conversation on the lighter side, she smiled and continued, "Grandpa Charley and I had a disagreement."

Mr. Flood smiled but didn't say anything. It was that same smile Grandpa Charley had when he was sure that he knew something you didn't. Finally, he broke the silence. "If you argued with Charley, you are among the few who ever did. What were you arguing about?"

"About Tony. Grandpa Charley's last wish was that I make things right with Tony, but I have no way of getting in touch with him."

"Let me tell you something about your Grandpa Charley."

"Mr. Flood, I appreciate it and I don't mean to be rude, but I really have to go."

"Well, that's up to you. If you need to leave, that's fine, but this is something you're gonna regret not knowing about Charley."

Mr. Flood was a kind man and he was slowly changing her mood just by getting her to talk about her feelings. Even beyond that, she was now intrigued.

"I guess I can stay for a little bit."

Mr. Flood smiled.

"That's more like it. Now, as I was sayin'."

Mr. Flood explained that there was a time when Grandpa Charley bailed the Flood family out of a serious jam. Heather had an idea of what he was talking about because his niece had mentioned it at the hospital. However, she had said that her uncle was never willing to share the full story with anyone. This made Heather even more interested.

Larry continued. In 1977, Larry Flood was living in the same house left to him by his parents, located behind the feed store. He agreed to mortgage the store and the house in order to help his brother build a modest home adjacent to the store on the same property. His wife was pregnant with their third child and the dilapidated single-wide trailer they lived in was no longer suitable. While Larry secured the financing from the bank, his brother was responsible for making the payment. At the time, this was not a problem because he had recently been promoted as a manager at the Holley Carburetor plant in Sallisaw. However, four years later, after a drunk driver took his life when their vehicles collided on Interstate 40, the responsibility of taking care of both families now weighed heavily and solely on the shoulders of Larry. Within the first year, he fell behind on the mortgage, which allowed the bank to increase the interest rate to 17.5%, despite never having previously been late on a payment. The bank was completely unwilling to provide any relief or assistance, which angered Larry as he came closer and closer to losing everything. Within weeks, the day came when Larry sold his last bag of feed. He seriously considered packing up his family and his brother's family and leaving the property. Yet they had nowhere else to go.

"Heather, foreclosure was absolutely inevitable. It would have been difficult to pay what I owed for the two months that I was behind, but it was impossible to keep up with the compounding interest. I felt like the bank set us up to fail from the beginning by putting a provision in our loan documents that allowed them to increase the interest rate. As that last customer left, I followed him outside, sat down on the ground and buried my face in my hands. I sat there and prayed for a miracle that I was certain would never come. Then your granddad pulled up in that old Chevrolet pickup. Until that day, I had only known him as a customer. But that day, he became more than my customer, he became my friend."

Most people in Sequoyah County had heard of Charley. He was known to frequent the library and courthouse, researching the location of old railroad lines and stage coach routes. Some people thought he was an eccentric history buff, while others believed him to be the long lost son of infamous outlaw Charles Arthur Floyd. Yet most people dismissed the rumors as false since they were based on the mere coincidence that Charley's middle names were the same as the outlaw's. Regardless, it was obvious that he was looking for "Pretty Boy Floyd's" long lost loot, which everyone believed to be a lost cause.

When Charley pulled up to the feed store, Larry stood up and told him that he had a bit of fuel left but he was completely out of feed. Larry dropped his head and told Charley that he would have to go into town to get feed for his cattle. He then sat back down on the ground and could not bring himself to look Charley in the eye. Charley got out of the truck and sat down next to Larry.

"Well, Larry, I'm sorry to hear that. I could have solved both our problems if I could have just figured out where the old Kansas City Southern rail line crossed a large creek, parallel to the old stagecoach road near a spring fed well and two unmarked graves.

The problem is that there is no historical information regarding the exact location of the railroad before it was moved or where the old stagecoach line used to run through Sequoyah County. And, as you know, creeks in this county number almost as many as people."

"Are you talking about the old ghost bridge?"

Charley's eyes widened.

"Not that I know of. I've been researching the railroad line for years and I've never heard of it."

"Well, you wouldn't have. Before my pa opened the store here, he worked for the Arkansas Oklahoma Gas Corporation. For several summers, as a teenager, I worked with him to make a few dollars and help with family expenses. He was responsible for the crew that ran the natural gas pipeline from Arkansas through Sequoyah County into Muskogee County. The line runs through the old berm of the Kansas City Railroad line. To my knowledge, the line only paralleled the old stagecoach road for a couple of miles and it crosses Little Sallisaw Creek, near South Dogwood Avenue. Before relocating the rail line further north, the railroad built an iron bridge that crossed the creek there in the late 1800's. It was later known as the old ghost bridge after the railroad abandoned the property and AOG tore most of it down in the 1950's. Part of the original structure is still there."

"If you can take me there, I just might be able to save your store. The only condition is that you can never mention this again, under any circumstance, to anyone, ever, including me."

"Mister, if you have any way to save my home and store, I'll do anything you ask."

"Get in. I'll drive."

Larry had nothing to lose. He locked up the store and directed Charley to the property. After hearing Charley describe the location he was looking for, it reminded Larry of a local legend he heard as a boy.

It was rumored that after robbing the bank in Sallisaw in November of 1932, with his mother watching on a nearby bench, authorities were close to catching up with Pretty Boy Floyd. In an effort to hide his stolen cache, he purportedly threw several bags of money down a local well and ditched his vehicle in the Illinois River shortly after taking a fellow bank robber to see his dead father at a funeral home. The rumors regarding the stolen money were believed to be false because, within days of the robbery, the FBI arrived in Sallisaw and dug up every well in the area but nothing was ever recovered. Larry couldn't help but wonder if they might have overlooked something and if Charley really might have known the whereabouts of the stolen cash. Larry sure hoped he did and, if so, he hoped that Charley was willing to help him out of his predicament.

Charley and Larry pulled up to the old wood-planked cabin on the property. Charley explained to the owners, Jamie and Misty Phillips, that they wanted to search for arrowheads. This was not an unusual request. People from all over Northeast Oklahoma hunted for arrowheads in streams and freshly tilled fields. There was an abundance of them since Oklahoma was designated as the final destination of the Trail of Tears between 1830 and 1850.

Mr. Phillips owner granted Larry and Charley permission to search for arrowheads with the understanding that if they found a flint carved thunderbird, they would turn it over to the property owner as payment. It was the Holy Grail for arrowhead collectors and the last piece the property owner needed to finish his collection. Larry and Charley agreed. They turned to walk away and then Charley turned back around. "One last thing. Does there happen to be an old cemetery of sorts on your property?"

"No. Nothing like that. I've been told that there were once two small unmarked gravestones in the pasture but I've never found them. No need to bother with them anyhow. They ain't Native American. I was told they belonged to the original homesteader's wife and daughter but my wife does not want them disturbed. She's Native American and funny about stuff like that. For example, every time she sees an owl, she believes something bad is going to happen."

Charley immediately knew that he had finally found the place he had been looking for.

"Thank you, Mr. Phillips. We'll find you a thunderbird to complete your collection."

"Good luck. We've been looking for years and only ever seen two from other people's collections."

Charley and Larry got back in the truck. Larry pointed in the direction of the old ghost bridge but not a word was said. They parked near the structure and gazed upon what little remained of the old railroad bridge. Larry remembered thinking that Charley was as excited as a child on Christmas morning. Charley pulled a yellowed brittle piece of paper from his wallet and unfolded it. He walked over to the center beam of the bridge and placed his back against it. He then walked due south, counting his paces out loud. Larry followed closely behind. Charley counted 222 paces before arriving at a deep depression in the ground. Charley bent down and placed his hand in the center of the depression.

"Charley, do you think this could have been the old well?"

Charley put his hand up, as if he were trying to concentrate. He stood back up, turned west and again began walking but this time silently, intent on the direction he was going. They walked for nearly a thousand yards before stopping. Charley bent down and uncovered two relatively thin marble slabs. They were gravestones that had fallen over, lying face down and covered with several inches of earth. Larry wondered how he even saw them. Charley reached down and lifted the first marble gravestone. He studied it closely, running his hand over both sides. It was blank, just as the property owner had described. Charley slowly lowered it back to the ground and lifted the second, carefully brushing the dirt away and examining both sides with his hand.

"It's really there."

Charley pointed to several tiny chiseled letters at the bottom of the gravestone:

"XX-III-I-III"

"What is it, Charley?"

"Roman numerals."

"Do you have any idea what they mean?"

"They correspond with letters of the alphabet. 20-3-1-3 or T-C-A-C, meaning Tony Charles Arthur Crambrink."

"I had always heard that the money was buried in a well."

"Because that's what dad wanted everyone to think so they wouldn't find it. And, hopefully, it worked."

Larry was shocked. They really were Charley's initials. Larry immediately knew the rumors were not rumors. They were true. *He really is Charles Floyd's son*, Larry thought to himself. They went back to the truck and pulled out a pick and a shovel and began digging. They dug for hours and then, about five feet below the surface, Charley hit something hard with the shovel. By that time, the sun was setting and they were covered in dirt and sweat. They dug around the edges, careful not to damage the homemade wooden coffin. Larry was nervous as Charley used the pick to pry the lid open. He didn't want any part of disturbing dead bodies, especially of a mother and her child. Charley reached in and pulled a large canvas bag from inside. He told Larry to hurry up and have the hole filled before he got back. Charley left and Larry filled the hole back in but was nervous that Charley might not return. Then Larry saw headlights bouncing across the pasture.

"I wasn't sure you were coming back."

"A deal is a deal. You held up your end and tomorrow morning I will hold up my end. But first we have to satisfy the property owners so they never investigate what happened here."

"What do you mean?"

"I'm going to give them what they asked for."

Charley reached in his shirt pocket and pulled out a flint carved thunderbird. He stopped by the Phillips' house on the way out and presented it to them. They were thrilled and couldn't thank them enough. Charley dropped Larry back off at the store.

"Larry, I'll be back first thing in the morning. Don't open the store until after I get here. I want to make sure we are alone."

"Well, that's no problem. There's nothing to sell anyway."

Larry hoped that Charley would be true to his word. When he got home, Larry's wife took one look at her filthy husband and asked him where he had been. He told her that he couldn't talk about it but that everything would be taken care of in the morning. She didn't understand but she trusted her husband. Larry didn't sleep a wink that night. The next morning he sat waiting in front of the store and, true to his word, Charley returned and handed Larry $25,000 cash. It was a humbling experience for Larry to take the money but he knew that he had no choice. *Besides, just like Charley said, a deal is a deal*, Larry told himself.

"Hey, Charley. Where did you get that thunderbird anyway?"

Charley smiled and said, "The less you know, the better."

They both laughed and Charley drove away. Larry paid off the bank that very day and never mortgaged the property again.

"Heather, I promised your Grandpa Charley I would never tell anyone about the events of that night and I never have until now. Charley quickly became my best friend and I never charged him for anything, even when he tried to pay. Out of respect for him, I will never charge you either so, like I told you, put that $20 bill back in your purse."

Heather reluctantly put the money back in her wallet. She now fully understood Grandpa Charley's connection to Mr. Flood and why his niece had allowed her back inside the hospital. She thanked Mr. Flood and filled her car up with fuel. As she drove home, she realized that she had a lot more to think about than she previously realized. She did not want to make the wrong decision about moving back to Louisiana or feel guilty about it later. Heather came to the realization that she had to make the conscious decision to move forward with fulfilling her promise to Grandpa Charley or give it all up forever and leave Oklahoma as planned. She again questioned how Grandpa Charley could really know the things he shared with her or how she would ever contact Tony. Heather fully understood what Grandpa Charley's expectations of her were but it was following through with them that was nearly impossible, she thought. And, while it really didn't matter, Heather could not help but wonder what happened to all of the money that Grandpa Charley pulled from the coffin.

CHAPTER 6

Tony was suddenly jolted back to reality as a flight attendant smiled and picked his boarding pass up off the floor. He hadn't even noticed he'd dropped it. Tony unclenched his fist, not realizing that he had it clenched in the first place. He reached out and took the boarding pass, attempting to thank her, but was unable to speak. Tony picked himself up out of the chair and barely made his connection to Houston. His jaw was clenched so tightly that he thought his teeth would crack. He forced his emotions as far from the surface as possible and refused to cry. *For what*, he thought to himself. *What was done was done and there was no changing it.* Attempting to satisfy his insatiable guilt, he justified that it wasn't his fault that he had not spent more time with Grandpa Charley. *After all, if my dad had not taken up with the local camp follower, I would have been allowed to visit Grandpa Charley over the years.* But now, with Grandpa Charley gone, he could be done with the whole lot of them, he thought to himself.

After arriving at the airport in Houston, Tony walked off the jetway and saw Oak. He had forgotten that they were planning to meet up. Tony had been looking forward to catching up with Oak but now all he wanted was to return to Venezuela.

"Hey, Tony. It's great to see you."

Tony was very dismissive and walked right past Oak.

"Come on, Oak. Let's get out of here. I'm in a hurry. I'm not going to be able to complete the training as planned. Something has come up and I have to get back to Venezuela."

"What happened?"

"It's none of your concern. I just have to get back. That's all."

"Come on, man. Let's at least go out for a night on the town."

"No, thanks."

"Fine, Tony. Don't worry about me. I had plans for us but you obviously got a better offer. I guess I'll see you later -- or I won't."

"Oak, it's not that. I just don't feel like talking right now."

"Yeah. Whatever. I'll be seeing you."

Tony knew that he had hurt Oak. Oak had moved from Venezuela to Williston, South Dakota the year before after accepting a promotion. Tony missed their weekend adventures. The gasoline in Venezuela was literally cheaper than water,

70

averaging $.04 per gallon, which made air and ground transportation within the country nearly free. Venezuela was an ecotourist's paradise and Oak and Tony took full advantage. It was not unusual for them to find themselves scuba diving at Morrocoy National Park, sand boarding the deserts of Los Médanos, base jumping off of Angel Falls, or hang gliding off of Pico Bolivar, Venezuela's tallest mountain peak.

Even on the rare occasion that they did not travel on their days off, adventure seemed to find them. For example, Oak and Tony had a double date planned with two beautiful Venezuelan women who had been introduced to them by a local vendor. They agreed to meet the women at the Plaza de la República in Maracaibo at 9:00 p.m. After the taxi dropped them off, Oak and Tony were robbed at knifepoint and the ladies were nowhere to be found. They immediately knew that they had been set up. However, one of the security measures taught by Halliburton security staff was to carry a separate cash roll, known as a "rob fund," with several small denominations of money rubber banded together with a larger denomination bill on the outside. The total value of the rob fund was approximately $20. As instructed, Tony handed the thief his rob fund and the thief took off running. He and Oak looked at each other, instantly knowing what the other was thinking. Simultaneously, they took off sprinting and chased down the assailant. Oak punched him and knocked the glasses from his face, while Tony grabbed him by the arm and removed the small canvas bag containing the knife. The man started begging them in Spanish not to hurt him. He told them that he would be killed if he returned to his employer empty handed. Tony pulled the cash from his pockets, including the rob fund, and they released him, although they kept the glasses and knife as trophies.

Tony collected his rental car in Houston and drove to the hotel. He checked in and sent an email to Halliburton's training supervisor and copied his direct supervisor, Rich. Tony requested an immediate return to Venezuela due to a death in the family and requested to complete the training at some future time. Tony turned on the TV and waited for a reply, hoping that it would come sooner than later.

Within a few hours, he received a response requesting additional information. The training supervisor wanted to know who had passed away, if the date of the funeral conflicted with the training and why the death of a family member in the U.S. necessitated a return to Venezuela. Tony immediately responded, explaining that he had just learned of the passing of his grandfather and that the funeral had been two months earlier. He just wanted to get back to work.

This time, the reply took twenty minutes. It was from Tony's direct supervisor, Rich. He bluntly told Tony that the training was not only mandatory but long overdue. Furthermore, since it did not interfere with any funeral plans, Tony would be required to attend as planned. He also explained that he would authorize Tony a week off immediately upon completing the training to get his head back where it needed to be.

Tony was furious. Grandpa Charley had always told him that if he wanted to play hard he had to work hard. As a result, Tony was a dedicated employee and worked hard. Yet in his hour of need, Rich refused to grant the only request he had ever made. Tony seriously contemplated quitting but he knew that was not the answer. He decided to get some sleep. He knew he would be able to think through things more clearly when he was not jetlagged and tired.

The next morning Tony woke up rested but he didn't feel any better. The hotel room phone rang. Somehow, his mom had tracked him down. *She must have called Halliburton's Houston office and asked where he was staying*, he thought.

"Tony, are you OK? I was worried about you. Why didn't you ever call me back?"

"I've been busy. I'm here on business, as you know."

"How are you handling the death of your Grandpa Charley?"

"Come on, Mom. I haven't seen him in years. It's not that big of a deal."

However, she could tell by his tone and dismissive attitude that it was taking a toll on him. Tony lied and told her that he was in a meeting and would call her back. The truth was that he just didn't feel like talking. His mom figured as much since she had called him at the hotel. Tony hung up the phone and got ready for work. He endured the first day of training and then went straight back to the hotel room. Oak was still irritated with him. They had not spoken the entire day.

The next morning his phone rang again. Tony figured it was his mom calling again. However, he was completely unprepared for who was on the other end of the line. It was his grandma, Patty. His mother had called to inform her that Tony was back in the country and was not handling the news of his Grandpa Charley very well. Patty attempted to comfort Tony. "Tony, I wish you could have been there. The funeral was beautiful and the chapel was overflowing with people that Grandpa Charley had influenced over the years. Grandpa Charley's casket was beautifully plain, made of stained wood. It looked like something he would have made himself."

At first, Patty was patient with Tony given the difficult circumstances. However, Tony was rude and condescending. "Yeah, Grandma, that's great. Sorry I missed it, but as you know, I was halfway around the world trying to make a living."

Patty ignored the snide comment and continued. "They held a 21-gun salute, something your Grandpa Charley would have been deeply touched and honored by."

"Don't you think I know that? I may not have been around as often as I would have liked but having been his namesake and his first grandson, I think I was as close to him as anyone."

By her tone, Tony could tell that his grandma was becoming agitated.

"Is there anything of your Grandpa Charley's that you would like to have?

"Nope. I've got everything I need and I'm doing just fine. Besides, I'm headed back to Venezuela just as soon as my training is over."

By this point Patty had gotten Tony's not so subtle hints. It was obvious that he had no desire to talk to her.

"OK, Tony. Bye." Patty hung up the phone. She had had enough.

Tony was now running late for training. He arrived at Halliburton's Corporate Campus and ran to his class. As he walked in the back door, he noticed Rich sitting toward the front. Tony took a seat in the back, hoping that Rich had not noticed that he was late. As the instructor went on, it was difficult for Tony to focus. He tried not to think of Grandpa Charley. However, the more he attempted to control his thoughts, the more they took over. As a result, Tony didn't get much out of the training but at least another day was over.

Unfortunately for Tony, everyone in his assigned group, including the instructor, noticed that he was disengaged. However, because Rich had not interacted with Tony up to that point, he hadn't noticed anything unusual. That evening Rich had dinner with the instructor. The instructor asked Rich about Tony. "What's up with Crambrink?"

"What do you mean?"

"Well, he hasn't participated in any of the group exercises for the past two days and today he was late."

"I hadn't thought to pay much attention to Tony but I guess it stands to reason."

"What do you mean?"

"When he arrived in Houston, he found out about the passing of his grandfather. I denied his request to forgo the training and go back to Venezuela after he emailed the Training Supervisor. It's nothing to worry about. I'll take care of it in the morning."

"What are you going to do?"

"What I always do. I'm going to solve the problem. He's getting a week off whether he likes it or not. He can make the choice to take it as vacation or mandatory leave without pay. Afterward, he will begin the training again before returning to Venezuela."

The next morning, true to his word, Rich was waiting for Tony in the classroom.

"Tony, step outside with me."

"No problem. Let me sign in first."

"There's no need. The instructor tells me that you aren't doing well in the training. Because I know that isn't like you and you are going through some things, I don't plan to take disciplinary action against you. However, I've approved a week off for you to do whatever it is you need to do to get your head screwed on straight and get back here to get trained."

"Rich, I'm doing fine. Time off is the last thing I need."

"Tony, you can either take the time off or it will be mandatory time off without pay."

"This is ridiculous."

Tony knew that once Rich had made up his mind, there was no changing it. Tony left, irritated. By the time Rich walked back into the classroom, the instructor had already begun. Oak noticed Rich smirking when he walked back in alone and he knew from personal experience what that meant. Oak had seen him in the hallway speaking with Tony. At the first break, Oak planned to confront Rich.

Tony drove away from the Corporate Campus feeling indifferent, disconnected and empty. Time off was the last thing he needed, he thought to himself. He had no idea what he was going to do with a week off. Unfortunately, he couldn't just stay at his hotel because Halliburton would not pay for his room while on vacation. He was so angry with Rich.

All of a sudden, all of the raw emotion that Tony had suppressed came rushing out. His futile attempt to hold it all together exploded in a gut wrenching flow of tears and a cry that barely sounded human. It was so bad that he could no longer see the roadway and had to pull the car onto the shoulder. For the first time since learning of Grandpa Charley's passing, Tony admitted that he missed his Grandpa Charley. Yet nothing he did could give him back the time he threw away to pursue his education or his career. He would have traded both for just one more day with his Grandpa Charley. As Tony sat there on the side of the highway, vehicles whizzing by, he lost control of his thoughts and his mind drifted back to the farm.

Before doing the morning chores, he and Grandpa Charley always ate fried eggs with mustard, biscuits with honey butter, and fried salt meat. Grandpa Charley drank his coffee from a dark orange Army issued coffee cup that he used at every meal. That's when it hit him. *There is something of Grandpa Charley's that I want.* Tony wiped the tears from his face and drove straight to the hotel to call his grandma. She answered the phone and, as hard as Tony tried, he knew that Grandma detected the emotion in his voice. She always sensed a person's vulnerability.

When Tony was eight years old, Grandpa Charley gave him his first pocketknife. It was an Old Timer with two blades. Grandma told Grandpa Charley several times, in front of Tony, not to give it to him because he would cut himself, but Grandpa Charley always did what he wanted. Tony felt so grown up because he had a pocketknife just like Grandpa Charley's.

That evening, Tony sat on the living room carpet in front of the TV with his new knife. Grandma and Grandpa Charley were sitting in their recliners behind him, watching an episode of Dallas. Tony opened the smaller blade and ran his finger along the sharp edge just as he had seen Grandpa Charley do a hundred times. However, Tony immediately felt a quick burning sensation as blood ran down his finger and into the palm of his hand. The pain was severe yet he held back the tears. He did not dare let Grandma know that he cut his finger, especially after Grandpa Charley had taken up for him. Tony glanced back at them and Grandma blurted out, "You cut yourself, didn't you?"

Tony started crying and, in one seamlessly single motion, Grandpa Charley scooped Tony out of the floor and headed down the hallway toward the bathroom.

"Don't worry, Number Two. We'll fix you right up."

Tony could still hear Grandma yelling in the background:

"I told you not to give him that knife, Charley. I told you he'd cut himself but you just don't listen. You're as hardheaded as a redheaded peckerwood."

Grandpa Charley ignored her and cleaned up Tony's cut. Grandpa Charley always knew just what to do to make things better.

But now he was gone and there was no making it better.

"Grandma, I'm sorry for the way I talked to you yesterday. I know there's no excuse but I just feel guilty for not being there when Grandpa Charley died."

"Don't worry about it. But thank you. You're still my grandson and I love you."

"I've had some time to think about some of Grandpa Charley's things that I would like to have if it's still OK."

"Of course it is. What would you like?"

"Well, if they're available, I'd like to have Grandpa Charley's coffee cup because it was something that he used every day. I would also like his leather wallet and his dog tags from the Army that I played with as a kid."

Grandpa Charley's wallet was custom made. It had his cattle brand burned into the leather, which consisted of Grandpa

Charley's initials, a large letter C, with a smaller letter T in the middle of the letter C. Grandma agreed to let him have the items with one stipulation:

"You have to come to Oklahoma to get them."

Patty didn't think this was too much to ask, especially because Tony had not been there for the funeral. She understood why, but she also believed that regardless of the reasons, it was his duty as a grandson to be there. In her mind, showing up to get the items he requested was the least he could do. Besides, it had been years since he had visited and she really wanted to see him.

Tony was infuriated. He had no plans of ever going back to Oklahoma, especially now that Grandpa Charley was gone. All he wanted were three worthless items. Things that no one else obviously wanted or they would have already been taken.

"That's great, Grandma. The next time I happen to pass through Oklahoma I'll be sure to pick them up."

Tony hung up the phone. It had never been a secret that Grandpa Charley and Grandma argued over almost everything. However, Tony could not believe that even after Grandpa Charley was dead, Grandma rejoiced in keeping something from happening that Grandpa Charley would have wanted. It reminded Tony of a time from his childhood.

It was a Saturday evening. Grandpa Charley was driving the three of them to Roger's Mountain Music when Grandma started arguing with him. Tony wasn't sure what the argument was about but as it began to intensify, Grandpa Charley looked down at Tony sitting between them. He immediately stopped arguing and then smiled and nodded in the affirmative to pacify Grandma and stop the argument. Later that night, while Grandma was in the bathroom, Grandpa Charley told Tony that in order to calm an angry woman, sometimes you just had to smile and nod.

Tony went back to the hotel and tried to relax by watching some television but he was not interested in anything that was on. He opened his laptop and started looking for destinations where he could spend the next week relaxing. He considered the beach in Cancun or fly fishing in Montana. However, he knew that no matter where he went, there was no way he was going to enjoy himself. He slammed the laptop closed and decided not to waste his money. He laid down on the bed and fell fast asleep.

Tony dreamt that he was back on the farm. He walked up to Grandpa Charley's back porch and walked in the back door. Grandpa Charley was sitting at the table in his usual spot.

"Sit down, my boy."

Tony sat down at the table next to Grandpa Charley.

"There is something very specific that I have saved for you."

"What is it, Grandpa Charley?"

"Follow me and I'll show you."

They walked outside to the side of the house and Grandpa Charley pointed directly north.

"My boy, the thing you desire is in that direction. If you'll have a little faith and follow the breadcrumbs, you will not only find what you're looking for but you will recognize it when you see it."

When Tony woke up, he wasn't sure how to feel. Strangely, his anger seemed to have been stripped from him. The dream seemed so real. He wanted it to be real. Tony desperately wanted to have whatever it was that his Grandpa Charley had saved for him. Tony wondered why Grandpa Charley hadn't just shown him what it was. He also wondered what Grandpa Charley meant by "Follow the breadcrumbs."

As much as he didn't want to, Tony knew what he had to do. As he packed, it was difficult for him to believe that he was actually going back. Nevertheless, he had to find out if Grandpa Charley had really spoken to him, and going back to Oklahoma was the only way to do that.

Suddenly, there was a knock at the door but Tony didn't answer. He figured it was someone with the wrong room because everyone he knew in the area was in training. What he didn't know is that it was Oak. Given the first opportunity, Oak had gone to Rich to inquire as to Tony's whereabouts:

"Rich, what did you do to Tony?"

"It's really none of your business, but if you must know, I sent him on a little vacation."

Rich smiled, unwilling to conceal his amusement.

"What did he do? Why'd you make him take time off if he's supposed to be in training with the rest of us?"

"Calm down, Oak. His grandfather passed away last month and he didn't find out until he landed in Curacao. I've given him some time off to take care of things."

82

Oak felt horrible for the way he had treated Tony. He wanted to be there for him. Against his better judgment, Oak lowered his guard and changed his tone. "I'll be back in a bit. I want to make sure Tony's OK."

"No. You need to be here just like the rest of us."

Trying to appeal to Rich's humanity didn't work as Oak had hoped. Without missing a step, Oak's wall came right back up. He remembered his own grandfather telling him that missed opportunities were the source of his greatest regrets and Oak was determined not to let that happen to him. Tony was his best friend and Oak was going to do whatever was necessary to make sure he was OK.

"Well, Rich, I'm sure you have my best interest in mind in counseling me to stay, but I think I'll leave anyway."

"If you do, I'll report you."

"Rich, do your worst. Or go to Hell. I don't care. It's the little things in life that matter, not classrooms and Powerpoint presentations. Maybe I could be higher up the ladder if I changed my attitude but I'm pretty high up as it is and I'm happy with that. Can you say the same?"

Oak walked out, content for having the last word. He used to tolerate Rich when he was his supervisor but that was no longer the case. Oak had wanted to tell Rich off for as long as he had known him. He had no doubt that Rich would report him but he knew that he would make the day up later, just as if he had missed the day for being sick. But after knocking on Tony's hotel room door and getting no answer, he figured that he had already missed Tony. With no way to contact him, Oak went back to training but immediately changed his travel plans. He was supposed to fly back to North Dakota on Friday after training. However, there was no way he was leaving without knowing that his best friend was all right.

CHAPTER 7

A representative of the moving company had left Heather a voicemail confirming that the movers would be there by 10:00 a.m. the next morning to load her things. It was sooner than she had expected and there was still some packing she had left to do. *I will be ready,* Heather told herself. The representative also explained that she should expect the truck to take between two and three days to deliver everything to her apartment in Baton Rouge. She had not even seen the apartment yet but it was within walking distance to LSU. *It was perfect,* she thought, awkwardly feeling like she was trying to convince herself. Her interview had reminded her that moving back to Baton Rouge meant facing some demons from the past, but in time, she thought she could handle that. After all, Baton Rouge was the one place she had always wanted to end up.

Finally, Heather packed the last of the boxes before heading out. She made the short drive to Akins to see Mr. Flood one last time. He was not expecting her but she wanted to thank him for sharing Grandpa Charley's story with her, especially because she knew that she might never see him again. Heather arrived at the store and walked in.

"Good morning, Mr. Flood."

It was almost as if he'd been expecting her.

"Good morning, Heather."

"Listen, I just wanted to thank you for sharing Grandpa Charley's story with me the other day. It meant a lot and it filled in some of the gaps that Grandpa Charley left out that night in the hospital."

"Well, he swore me to secrecy but I figure the worst he can do now is haunt me."

They both laughed.

"Something I failed to tell you is that I am moving away and I wanted to say goodbye."

"Oh yeah? Where you headed?"

"Back home to Baton Rouge."

"So I guess you feel like your work here is complete?"

"What do you mean?"

"Knowing your granddad the way I did, I suspect he had a few things he wanted you to do for him after he passed away."

"What is it with you people? How would you possibly know that?"

"Well, a little birdie may have told me. Mr. Williford happens to be my attorney also."

"What happened to attorney/client privilege?"

"Heather, just because you got a letter from Charley doesn't mean that you were the only one who got one."

Instantly, Heather knew that Mr. Flood had been part of Grandpa Charley's plan all along and she had played right into it. She smiled, knowing Grandpa Charley had gotten her again.

"Well, Mr. Flood, what if I hadn't stopped by the other day? The only reason I did is because I was nearly out of gas."

"Heather, dear, you just go on believing that, but regardless, you did stop by."

"I have done everything Grandpa Charley asked me to do, except talk to Tony and as I imagine you know, that's just not possible. I mean, he lives on another continent, for crying out loud."

"Have you asked Patty if she might have a way to contact him?"

"I'm sure that she doesn't because Grandpa Charley didn't have a number for him either. And no offense, Mr. Flood, but you obviously don't know her very well. There is no way she would tell me, even if she did have a way to contact him."

"I knew your Grandpa Charley better than most and one thing I do know about him is that he would have never asked you to do something that he believed was impossible."

Heather knew that he was right. *But what if Grandpa Charley is wrong,* she asked herself. It didn't matter. If she was to leave the next day with a clear conscience, she had to try. Heather hugged Mr. Flood and told him goodbye. Mr. Flood smiled and wished her luck on her journey. Heather wondered if he was referring to her journey to Baton Rouge or to Patty's house, because attempting a conversation with her was definitely the more difficult of the two. Never once had Heather been able to have a decent conversation with Patty.

Heather drove toward the farm for the last time, contemplating how she would approach Patty without it turning into a confrontation. She had no idea. The more she thought about it, the more her anxiety grew. Heather went on past the farm and stopped by Central Junior High first to speak with Mr. Wight. She still needed to inform him of her decision to follow through with her resignation. Heather walked in and Mr. Wight looked up and smiled.

"Good afternoon, Heather. Tell me you have changed your mind."

"I'm sorry, Mr. Wight, but I need to do this. Please don't make it any harder than it already is. I am so appreciative of all you have done for me but this is an amazing opportunity and, no offense to you personally, but there is just nothing left for me here."

Mr. Wight didn't say anything. He picked up a small stack of stapled papers lying on his desk and tore them up. He handed the torn pieces to Heather.

"I had a feeling you would say that. Here is the last remaining copy of your contract."

Mr. Wight stood up and hugged Heather, which was unusual because he had never hugged her before.

"We will miss you and you will always have a place here."

"Thank you so much, Mr. Wight."

Heather turned and walked away with tears in her eyes. Heather drove less than a mile north from the school and stopped at the edge of Grandpa Charley's farm. She wanted to take a few moments to feel his spirit and walk in his footsteps one last time before she took on the daunting task of speaking with Patty. However, the land felt different. It seemed devoid of any trace of Grandpa Charley.

All of a sudden, a light breeze tossed Heather's hair into her face. She closed her eyes and attempted to smell the sweet reminiscent aroma of honeysuckle but it was gone. The barbed wire fence once overgrown with honeysuckle had been replaced by a fancy metal pipe and cable fence. The tree house had been removed but the old metal ladder still stood against the tree, rusted and weathered, as if someone forgot to haul it off. The old fashioned mailbox bearing Grandpa Charley's name with ornate metal letters that matched Iron Post Corner, had been replaced by a cheap generic one, no doubt from Wal-Mart.

Heather walked past where Hank's trailer used to be and up to the back gate. The gate had withstood the test of time, even as so many other things had seemingly vanished. As she opened the latch, she was suddenly 12 years old again.

It was a warm summer night. Lightning bugs intermittently illuminated the darkness beyond the boundary of the vapor light that hung above the iron gate. Heather and Tony were jumping up, grabbing the top of the gate's frame and swinging forward, propelling themselves through the gate's opening. They had gone out back because Hank was on the front porch with his drinking buddies playing poker. You wanted nothing to do with Hank when he was drinking that much for that long, a lesson Tony and Heather learned the hard way that night.

As they took turns swinging through the gate, Tony got the bright idea to close the gate behind Heather as she swung through. Heather leapt through the metal frame to the other side and landed on the ground. As she turned around to watch Tony swing through again, the gate continued through the frame and struck her in the face, knocking her to the ground. Heather screamed as intense pain filled the left side of her face. Quickly realizing that Hank was out on the front porch, Heather jumped up and did her best to pull herself together. She put one hand on Tony's shoulder while the other covered her face. She could feel something warm between her fingers and she didn't know if it was her tears or blood.

"Tony, I will never tell anyone what happened. It was an accident and that's all anyone needs to know."

Before Tony could say anything, Heather ran toward home hoping Hank had not heard her scream, or at least chose to ignore it. However, that was not the case. Hank stumbled around the corner of the trailer just in time to see Heather running home with her hand covering her face.

"What happened?"

Heather didn't stop to answer. She just kept running. The next thing she heard was Tony screaming, "No, Dad! Please! I'm sorry!"

She could hear Hank beating Tony until she stepped inside. She ran to her room, threw her face in her pillow and sobbed. The pain she felt was no longer from the injury to her face but for the anguish she felt for Tony. Heather knew he had not meant to hurt her. For more than a week, Heather went over every day but, each time, Ellen told her that Tony wasn't feeling well. Heather and Tony never talked about that night. However, she could still feel the pain of that night as she reached up, grabbed the gate's frame and swung through. Heather caught herself wishing Tony were there to swing through the gate with her, until she quickly dismissed any such thoughts, reminding herself that her childhood friend no longer existed.

Heather continued in the direction of the barn but it was also gone. It had been destroyed by a small localized tornado within days of Grandpa Charley's passing. It was as if Grandpa Charley had come back with a vengeance and taken his barn with him. Heather could see him doing that. *He had a funny sense of humor*, she thought to herself.

Heather walked to the corner of the property where Miller Ridge Road intersected with Central High Road, the location of

Iron Post Corner. She put her hand on the warm metal surface, closed her eyes and softly whispered, "I miss you, Grandpa Charley. I hope you understand…"

Heather's thoughts were interrupted by a voice in the distance that she instantly recognized. It was Patty, "Hey. You're trespassin'. You ain't got no business here."

Heather wanted to correct Patty's use of the double negative "ain't got no," which actually meant Heather had business there. However, she knew that it would only escalate things.

"Please, Patty. Let me explain. I just need to ask if you have a way to contact Tony. Please. And then you'll never see me again."

"First of all, if you were looking for a favor, you pull down someone's driveway and knock on the door. You don't park at the edge of their property to hide your vehicle and walk around snooping. Second of all, even if I had his number, which I ain't sayin' I do, I wouldn't give it to you. It ain't my place. If he wanted to contact you, he would. Now get off my property or I'll call the law."

Heather walked back to her car, all the while unsuccessfully attempting to ignore Patty's rant. "You ain't welcome here. You hear me? Don't you come back now, you hear? You ain't wanted and you'll never be a Crambrink, no matter what Charley ever told you."

Heather never understood how Grandpa Charley put up with her. She began to cry as she drove away. It really bothered her that she let Patty get to her yet again. Heather felt like she had cried more in the last two months than she had in her entire life. Initially, after visiting the farm Heather planned to visit the cemetery one last time to give Grandpa Charley a proper goodbye. However, after her run-in with Patty, she just went home. *Patty had won again*, she thought.

Heather arrived home and plopped herself on the couch. She caught herself staring at the only picture of Grandpa Charley she had. It was sitting on the mantle above the fireplace. It was a picture of Grandpa Charley, Tony and Heather riding Big Boy, Boomer, and Sugar, Grandpa Charley's horses, in the Grand Entry of the annual Sallisaw rodeo. Heather reached over and picked up the copy of the Sequoyah County Times that she had saved, which was sitting on the end table. Grandpa Charley's obituary was inside. She pulled out the pocketknife that Grandpa Charley had given her and methodically cut out the article on the glass coffee table. She then carefully placed it between the glass and the frame of the rodeo picture. She thought about Grandpa Charley's words. He told her that by going to the cemetery each week she would find what she was looking for and that she would know exactly what that was. *Maybe he was talking about my new job*, she thought to herself but she just wasn't sure. She also didn't know what going to the cemetery had to do with her job but she convinced herself that it had to be what he was talking about.

That night, Heather couldn't sleep. She felt guilty for allowing Patty to upset her enough to change her mind about going to the cemetery. It was the last chance she had to say goodbye and now it was too late. The movers were arriving in the morning and she was leaving for Baton Rouge.

CHAPTER 8

As Tony neared Sallisaw he took Exit 308 off Interstate 40 rather than Exit 311 that would have taken him directly to Grandpa Charley's farm. He wanted to take the time to drive through Sallisaw since he had not been there in more than a decade. Some things had changed. However, most things remained the same. For example, Blue Ribbon Downs, the horse racing track, was permanently closed, the Farmer's Cooperative, where Grandpa Charley used to work, had moved out of town and the old Ben Franklin store was now a pawn shop.

Tony continued east on Highway 64 toward Fort Smith, Arkansas, before turning onto Central High Road. He slowed down as he passed the school. There was a new football field and several new buildings with a new fence all the way around the campus. It was sad, Tony thought, that it now looked more like a prison than a school. He crossed the railroad tracks and arrived at the farm.

Tony hadn't realized it but he had expected the farm to look exactly as it did when he was young. However, the barn was gone. The garden was unkempt with a large potbelly pig inside. The chicken coop was overgrown with weeds and devoid of chickens. His dad's trailer had been removed and it was as if his tree house had never been there.

Tony remembered when he and Grandpa Charley built the tree house. Grandpa Charley emphasized the importance of not hurting the tree. They built the entire tree house without putting a single nail into the tree. In every project they worked on, Grandpa Charley always told Tony that if he took care of his property, it would take care of him.

Tony slowly pulled down the narrow driveway and parked next to Grandpa Charley's truck. To his surprise, Grandpa Charley's workshop was also gone. They had spent as much time in the old shop as they did anywhere. Tony got out of his car and walked through the front yard to where the old Magnolia tree had once stood tall and strong. Now it was nothing more than a stump.

As a boy, Tony often climbed the Magnolia tree for fun. However, on one particular occasion, when he was nine years old, his dad embarrassed him in front of the whole family at Thanksgiving dinner. Tony took refuge in the tree to escape the horror caused by his dad. Within seconds, Grandpa Charley came out.

"Come on down here, Number Two."

Tony started to climb down and then decided to show off in front of Grandpa Charley by swinging from limb to limb like a monkey. All of a sudden, the limb Tony grabbed snapped and he came crashing down until the last branch caught his shirt and left him dangling about three feet off the ground. The branch scraped his back from his waist to almost his shoulders. He began crying and Grandpa Charley took him in and cleaned him up. *Grandpa Charley always took care of me no matter the circumstances*, Tony thought to himself.

Tony walked around to the back door where they normally came and went from, and saw the old catalpa tree. He and Grandpa Charley had gotten so many worms off the tree for fishing over the years. Tony looked up and saw the only remnant of the tire swing that once hung from the tree's largest branch. It was only a few feet of frayed rope too high to reach. He knocked on the back door, but to his surprise there was no answer. Tony wondered where Grandma could be. He decided to continue walking around the property until she got home. Tony continued to where his dad's trailer had once stood. A strong sense of betrayal came over him. He knew better than most what it was like to be led astray by those who were supposed to love and protect him. He remembered that last summer at his dad's.

Hank had picked Tony up at his mom's, as usual, but when they got home Ellen had locked herself in Tony's room and was sobbing loud enough for everyone to hear. Tony had no idea what was wrong with her but he was aware that she and his dad had been having problems for some time. When she finally came out, her face was beet red and she moved with the swiftness of a gazelle. She left with the clothes on her back and never returned. Almost immediately Tony was aware that his dad found comfort in the arms of a female friend that he had known since high school. At first, Tony's naivety had led him to be grateful for his dad's newly found happiness. However, he could never have predicted that his dad's relationship with that woman was about to take him to his Grandpa Charley's house for the very last time.

It was like any other Sunday and Tony looked forward to going to Grandpa Charley's house for lunch. Sundays were always a special treat because whenever they walked through the door, the wonderful aroma of Grandma's freshly cooked apricot fried pies filled the air. They always caused Tony's mouth to salivate uncontrollably until Grandma would finally let him "test" one.

However, what was different about that particular Sunday was that it was the first time Hank's female friend accompanied them to Grandpa Charley's for lunch. Looking back, Tony realized that it was the beginning of the end. Not a word was said during lunch. Before finishing his meal, Grandpa Charley stood up abruptly, scooted his chair back with his legs, and quickly walked into the living room. Hank jumped up and followed, as did Grandma and

Hank's female friend. Grandpa Charley started arguing with Hank because he was dating another woman while he was still married to Ellen.

"Hank, just what the hell is this?"

"Well, just what the hell does it look like?"

"It looks like you're committing adultery."

"Trust me. It's over between me and Ellen. We're all but divorced."

"You weren't raised that way and you're not having an affair while you're still married to another woman. Do you understand me? I don't care if you are getting divorced or not. You ain't divorced yet."

"Well, I've got news for you, pal. I'm a grown man and I'll do what I want. In fact, I have full intentions of marrying her."

Tony was shocked by what he saw next. Grandpa Charley punched Hank in the face and knocked him into the living room window, shattering it. Hank glared at Grandpa Charley and touched his face to see if he was bleeding. Hank then stormed back through the kitchen and out the back door.

"Come on, Tony. We're out of here."

Hank left the house with his female companion and Tony followed close behind. Tony walked out the back screen door and took one last look back at Grandpa Charley.

"I'm so sorry, Number Two. Please forgive me."

Grandpa Charley didn't have to ask for his forgiveness. Tony loved his Grandpa Charley and nothing could ever change that.

Besides, Tony figured that if Grandpa Charley punched his dad, his dad deserved it. That same day, the woman and her two children moved in with Hank and Tony. After that, Tony was no longer allowed to go to Grandpa Charley's or play with Heather. Tony knew better than to ask his dad why. Questioning him would have just meant being whipped with the belt. Besides, Tony's dad always told him, "Your duty is not to question why. Your duty is to do or die."

In reality, Hank believed Heather's family to be staunch supporters of what he referred to as "the old regime," which is why Tony was no longer allowed to see them. Two days after Hank's friend moved in, a Sequoyah County Sheriff's deputy showed up with the woman's husband and a court order to take their two kids from her. Later that evening Tony overheard her tell Hank that it wasn't fair for him to have visitation of his son if she could not see her children. The next morning was June 7th, a date forever burned into Tony's mind. Hank packed up the few clothes that Tony had, and he and his new fiancée drove Tony back to his mother's house. Nothing was said during the long, one-hour trip to Muskogee. When they pulled up in front of Tony's mother's house, Hank handed him a new video game as some sort of consolation prize.

"But Dad, I already have this game."

"Then save it and we'll exchange it the next time I see you."

Hank never returned. It was eight years before Tony finally threw the unopened video game away. He grew up not knowing what he had done to deserve to be abandoned by his father.

Tony returned to Grandma's back porch and knocked on the back door again. There was still no answer. He attempted to open the door but it was locked. *Strange,* he thought to himself. Tony couldn't remember that door ever being locked before. He wondered where Grandma would be at such a late hour. As much as he didn't want to, Tony decided to drive back into town to his uncle's house to ask if he knew where Grandma was.

Tony knocked on the door and an older lady who Tony had never met answered. Tony asked if his uncle was home and she said that he was working but asked if she could be of assistance. Tony asked if she knew where Patty Crambrink was. Her eyes widened as she took a deep breath.

"You're Hank's boy, aren't you? I've heard so much about you."

Tony forced out a laugh to be polite.

"Well, you can't believe everything you hear."

"Oh, no. I've only heard good things about you. It's nice to finally meet you."

She held her hand out for Tony to shake. Attempting to avoid an awkward moment, Tony quickly shook her hand and changed the subject.

"I went by Grandma's but she wasn't home. Do you know where she might be?"

"I know that sometimes during the day she goes home to check on things, but she's had some health issues lately so she's been living with your dad."

Tony's heart sank. *How could this be,* he asked himself. He had come such a long way and now it all seemed for naught. Tony thanked her and drove back toward the farm not knowing what his next step was. *However, there is no way I'm going to my dad's house,* he thought.

Tony realized that he would probably never come back to the farm, so he decided to walk around one last time to remember the good times with Grandpa Charley. Tony really missed him. As he walked around for the last time, he remembered just how good Grandpa Charley had been to him throughout his life. Tony looked up and saw the old cast iron dinner bell atop the pole that Grandma used to ring to summon him and Grandpa Charley back to the house for dinner. He reached up and grabbed the rope to hear the clang of the bell one last time but the rope snapped. It had rotted and the bell was obviously rusted in place.

Tony realized that since he was unable to see his grandma, he was not going to receive the items that Grandma had promised him, nor would he find whatever it was that Grandpa Charley had told him about in the dream. Disappointed, Tony decided that the dinner bell would have to do. *At least I'll have something tangible from the farm to remind me of Grandpa Charley,* he thought. He went into the garage and found an old rusty crescent wrench and a pair of pliers.

Tony somehow managed to reach the bell's rusty bolts by standing on top of the hedgerow and clinging to the pole. It took some doing but he unbolted the bell from the pole and it crashed to the ground, causing a loud clang that Tony knew from firsthand experience could be heard at least a mile away. Tony hoped his dad had not heard it on the back side of the property where he now lived. But just in case, Tony decided that it was time to leave. He put the bell in the trunk of his car and quickly walked to where he and Grandpa Charley had been standing in his dream. He looked north, back in the direction of the house, in the same direction that Grandpa Charley had pointed. Tony truly believed that Grandpa Charley had something to give him and he regretted not finding it. He also regretted not being able to visit Grandpa Charley's grave but he had no idea where Grandpa Charley was buried. Tony got in his car and took one last look at the farm through the rearview mirror before heading back to Houston.

Within the few seconds it took to get to Iron Post Corner, Tony grew furious with his dad and pulled over. Tony got out of the car and put his hand against the cold metal pole. He admired the craftsmanship of the metal sign, knowing that his grandpa had built it by hand. Grandpa Charley told him on more than one occasion that it was named Iron Post Corner by the locals. Grandpa Charley built it hoping that the sign would point tourists in the direction of Sequoyah's Cabin. So many of them stopped by his farm for directions, believing that they were travelling on Highway 101, which was another mile section north.

All of a sudden Tony decided that it was now or never. He got back in his car and drove toward his dad's house with no regard for the consequences. He had to know if the dream was real and, if it was, he wasn't going to let anything stop him from claiming what he believed was rightfully his, especially his dad.

As Tony drove up the hill on Miller Ridge Road, he could see his dad's house on the back end of Grandpa Charley's property. His stomach felt like it was tied in knots, his hands began sweating and he was extremely nervous. He had not heard from or spoken to his dad since that fateful day shortly after turning 14. Yet he felt that he owed it to Grandpa Charley and to himself to find out if the dream was true.

Tony drove down the quarter mile long driveway that seemed to go on forever. He parked, got out of the car and marched up to the house, refusing to let his dad win this one. Tony peered inside the entryway window to see his dad's wife and his grandma sitting on the couch watching TV. They had not noticed him yet but he was not about to turn around at this point. Tony knocked and his dad's wife answered the door. The years had not been kind to her, he thought to himself, as she looked much older than she was. She looked at Tony as if she did not recognize him.

"Can I help you?"

"I'm here to see Grandma."

Her expression changed as the realization dawned on her. She knew exactly who he was.

"Well, your dad's not here right now. He's out of town on business. And your Grandma is not feeling well."

Before she could continue, Tony's grandma pushed his dad's wife out of the way and gave Tony a big hug. Tony was immediately relieved.

"I've missed you, boy. I am so surprised to see you. After our last conversation, I didn't think you'd be coming back to Oklahoma, but I'm so glad you're here."

"Well, Grandma, you didn't give me much choice."

Grandma smiled, content with her clever self. It reminded Tony of when she used to have him cut a piece of yarn in half and then, somehow, she would chew the yarn back together, as if it had never been cut. Tony never did understand how she did that.

"Grandma, it's great to see you but I'm here to get the things that you promised me over the phone."

"Well, it's late, but if you are willing to come back tomorrow and pick me up, I will be glad to take you to the house and get the things you asked for."

Tony felt impatient but he understood.

"OK, Grandma. I'll see you tomorrow."

Tony turned to leave as Hank's wife called out to him:

"Tony, wait."

He turned around and she walked over to him.

"I'll let your dad know that you're back. I'm sure he would like to see you but I'm not sure that he can make it back for at least a couple of days. Will you still be in town?"

Tony was relieved that he would have time to get what he had come for and get out of town before his dad could make it back.

105

"I tell you what. I'm staying at the Days Inn and if Dad wants to see me, he can call me there before I leave."

"OK. I'll let him know."

The next morning Tony woke up bright and early. He decided to get his hair cut at Padgett's Barber Shop, just like he did when he was a kid. It was good to see Mr. Padgett but the strange thing was that he hadn't seemed to age a bit.

"Hello, Mr. Padgett. I don't know if you remember me but I'm..."

Mr. Padgett interrupted him. "I know who you are, son. Can't mistake a Crambrink when you see one."

He then gave Tony a warm smile.

"Now, jump up here in the chair and I'll give you a good once over."

They reminisced about the good old days and about Grandpa Charley. Tony thought it was so nice to talk to someone who not only cared but seemed to understand. Afterward, Tony headed back to his dad's house. Knowing that his dad was not there made it so much easier to drive down the driveway. Tony's grandma met him out front. She seemed impatient and almost irritated, as if she had been waiting for him.

"You finally ready to go, Tony?"

She was different than she had been the evening before. Tony didn't think that they had settled on a specific time but he wondered if maybe he was wrong.

"Is everything OK, Grandma?"

106

"Oh, it's just fine."

"Grandma, you seem irritated."

"I just don't know why you and your dad can't forget the past and get along."

Tony was silent the rest of the short drive to Grandma's house. Grandma had obviously had a conversation with his dad since their visit the night before.

"Your dad told me not to give you anything, but since you've come all this way and since I promised you those things, I will get them for you. But I don't know exactly where your grandpa's wallet is so you're going to have to wait while I find it."

"That's no problem at all, Grandma. Thank you. I really appreciate it."

Perfect, Tony thought to himself. It would give him the opportunity to look through the house and find whatever it was that Grandpa Charley had for him. Although Tony still hadn't figured out why Grandpa Charley took him outside to point back toward the house, Tony guessed that it really didn't matter. In the dream Grandpa Charley told him that he would recognize it when he saw it and Tony was determined to find whatever it was.

As Tony and Grandma walked into the house, a sense of comfort came over him that he hadn't felt in years. Nothing inside the house had changed. There was still the slight fragrance of Grandma's home cooking floating on the air as they entered the kitchen through the back door.

Grandma interrupted Tony's thoughts. "You sit down at the table while I find the wallet, and don't get up until I get back."

How strange, he thought. As a child he was allowed to go anywhere in the house, just as if he had lived there. But now, Grandma wasn't even allowing him to walk around the house. He had no idea how he was going to find whatever Grandpa Charley had for him if he couldn't roam freely around the house. Tony started to get frustrated, but as instructed, he sat down at the table. Of course, he chose Grandpa Charley's chair. It was next to the filing cabinet that doubled as a safe. It had been there as long as Tony could remember. He opened the first metal door and revealed the safe with the familiar bullet hole in the dial. Grandpa Charley told him that someone had broken into the house while they were out of town sometime in the 1960s. The thief broke into the safe but since Grandpa Charley did not keep anything of value inside, the burglar didn't get away with anything significant. At the time Grandpa Charley told Tony the story, he said that anything he had of real value was in his other safe. However, to Tony's knowledge, Grandpa Charley didn't have any other safe.

Tony could still hear Grandma rattling around in her room looking for Grandpa Charley's wallet, so he decided to get up and start looking around. He figured he would run back to the kitchen table undetected when he heard Grandma coming back down the hallway. Tony looked at family pictures on the shelves in the living room and saw his great grandmother's pocket watch hanging in a glass case next to her picture. Grandpa Charley once told Tony that it was one of the few things he owned that belonged to his mother. It was given to her as a gift from Grandpa Charley's father. That was the only time that Tony could recall Grandpa Charley ever mentioning his father. Later that same day, Tony asked Grandma about his Grandpa Charley's father. All she knew was that Grandpa Charley had met him a handful of times when he was young but she was not sure that Grandpa Charley even knew his name. However, she told Tony that the reason Grandpa Charley referred to him as his "little confederate" was because that was what his father called him the few times that Grandpa Charley could remember meeting him.

Wrapped up in his thoughts, Tony did not hear Grandma exit her bedroom. All of a sudden she appeared in the living room, visibly upset.

"What are you doing in here? I told you to stay at the table."

"I'm sorry, Grandma. I didn't think it was a big deal. I was just looking at these old photos of you and Grandpa Charley."

"Well, it is a big deal. Here is Grandpa Charley's wallet. It has everything in it that it did the day he passed. I guess I have no idea where his dog tags are. They weren't where they were supposed to be. Maybe your dad already got them."

Grandma handed Tony Grandpa Charley's wallet and then walked over to the cabinet and pulled Grandpa Charley's brown military-issued coffee cup from the shelf. She handed it to Tony. It was well used and still had the stain and odor of coffee inside. The bottom of the cup was stamped with the words, *"Republic Mold Corp, Chicago, Illinois, US."*

"Thank you, Grandma. Are you sure there is nowhere else you can look for Grandpa Charley's dog tags? I'd really like to have them."

"I thought I knew right where they were. They hung on the right corner of the mirror in Grandpa Charley's room for years but they weren't there. I guess I can go out to my sewing room and see if they may have been moved out there. We moved some of Grandpa Charley's things out there after he passed but this is the last time I'm gonna tell you. Go sit down at the table and don't get up again until I come back."

This was so unlike Grandma, he thought. He figured that his dad must have told her not to trust him. Tony sat back down at the table even more frustrated than before. He had no way of finding whatever it was that Grandpa Charley had saved for him, which meant that he had no way to confirm whether his dream of Grandpa Charley was real. Nevertheless, Tony chose to believe. He got up and quickly went to the back door where Grandpa Charley always kept a gun. Sure enough, Grandpa Charley's Browning 28-gauge shotgun hung on the wall in the gun rack. Tony took the gun and quickly concealed it outside under a bush so that he could return later to pick it up. *At least I'll have something that belonged to Grandpa Charley,* he thought.

Tony ran back in the house and sat back down at the table before Grandma caught him. While sitting at the table Tony thumbed through Grandpa Charley's wallet. Inside there was $43, several credit cards and four photos. Tony looked at each of the photos. He recognized Libby and Cindy, his cousins, and himself. It was his school picture from sixth grade. As he turned to the last photo, he did not immediately recognize it. The photo was of a young girl who looked vaguely familiar. He pulled the photo from the plastic sheet and read the back.

"Heather, 12 years old."

Tony remembered his childhood friend from summers long ago. It had been so long since he had thought of her. For a fleeting moment he wondered where life had taken her. When he was young, Heather had been one of the few people who understood him and that he trusted. Like Grandpa Charley, she had been one of the few constants in his life. He remembered talking to Grandpa Charley on the phone for the first time after graduating from high school and Grandpa Charley told him that Heather and her family had moved to Arkansas. Tony wished he had someone like her to confide in again. Someone who understood him and what he had been through.

Suddenly, Grandma came back into the kitchen. "Come here, Tony. I want to show you something."

Tony walked over to his grandma who was standing by the back door. She closed the door to reveal the gun rack.

"That's strange. I was going to show you the shotgun that my dad gave me but I guess Hank may have already taken that too. Oh well. Go ahead and sit back down at the table. I have a few more places I can look."

Tony sat at the dining room table feeling horrible for what he had done. Tony ran outside, grabbed the shotgun and propped it up behind the door, rather than putting it back in the gun rack, before sitting back down at the table.

"Grandma. Come here."

Grandma returned to the kitchen.

"What is it?"

"Grandma, I just looked behind the door and there is this old shotgun leaning against the wall. Is this the one you were talking about?"

"Yes. That's it. Strange that it's standing in the corner rather than hanging in the gun rack where it belongs."

She picked up the shotgun and handed it to Tony.

"One day while my dad and I were out dove hunting, he bet me that I couldn't hit a dove that was sitting on a tree branch about twenty yards away. He handed me his shotgun and I hit it. We ate the dove for dinner and he gave me the shotgun as a prize for such a great shot."

"That's awesome, Grandma. I appreciate you sharing that with me, really."

"Now sit back down at the table and let me finish looking for those dog tags. They have to be around here somewhere."

Tony sat back down. Out of sheer boredom he began looking through the filing cabinet. He found Grandpa Charley's old Timex watch and his favorite set of red Bakelite dominos. As thrilled as Tony was to have found those items, he was pretty sure that they were not the items he was looking for. Grandpa Charley had told him in the dream that he would recognize it when he found it. He continued his search to no avail, failing to locate anything of significance. Grandma snuck back into the kitchen and peeked through the doorway to ensure that Tony had not gotten up from the table. Tony saw her looking through the doorway and jumped back out of the filing cabinet, unsure if she had caught him or not.

Grandma was not sure what he was doing but because of the way he jumped when he saw her, she was sure he was up to something. *At least he's sitting at the table like he's supposed to be,* she thought.

"Grandma, I found Grandpa Charley's Timex watch. It doesn't work but I'd still like to have it if that's OK."

"We'll have to ask your dad first and make sure that it's not something he wants."

This irritated Tony. He knew that even though his dad had zero interest in the watch, he would never agree to give anything to Tony. That last summer, before they had taken him back to his mom's house, Grandpa Charley gave Tony a Winchester 30-30 rifle. Hank immediately took the rifle from Tony and told him that he was not old enough to have a rifle and that Grandpa Charley should have never given it to him in the first place.

The summer before that, Grandpa Charley gave Tony a newborn baby calf to raise during the summer with the intent of selling it at the cattle auction early in the fall. Tony named him Fred and fed him every day that summer. Fred grew into a healthy young steer. Grandpa Charley took Tony to the auction where Fred was sold for over $400. When he got back to his dad's house that evening, his dad made Tony hand the money over for "safekeeping." Tony never saw the money again.

Tony's experience of his dad was that he had never let him keep anything that was rightfully his. Therefore, there was no doubt in Tony's mind that his dad would ever agree to let him have anything. Grandma left Tony and went back to her sewing room to finish looking for the dog tags.

It wasn't long before Tony arrived at the bottom drawer of the filing cabinet. It was just like the top drawer, full of miscellaneous papers, which almost caused Tony to close the drawer without looking through it. However, Tony started pulling the papers out of the filing cabinet and began stacking them on the table. All of a sudden, he noticed a brown object poking out from under a stack of papers toward the back of the drawer. Tony reached in and pulled out a vintage knife with a six-inch blade. The leather sheath was cracked and the snap was broken. Tony pulled the knife from the sheath and observed a well-used but well cared for "Cattaraugus" brand knife. Tony took a closer look at the sheath and observed the words, *"To my love, Tony Charles Arthur Crambrink - Promoted to First Sergeant by Colonel Jack Rose - presented by Annie, August 30, 1942"* etched into the leather sheath. He had never seen this knife before but an object of such a

114

personal and historical significance to their family and to Grandpa Charley had to be what Grandpa Charley was saving for him. If it was, he still wondered why Grandpa Charley didn't just show it to him in the dream rather than taking him back outside and pointing back in the direction of the house. Tony put all of the papers back into the drawer just before Grandma came back into the kitchen.

"You didn't get up, did you?"

Tony rolled his eyes.

"No, Grandma. You told me to sit here and not move, remember?"

"I was just making sure."

While they conversed, Tony had his arms under the table. He discreetly slipped the knife, dominoes and watch into his pants. He hated the idea of taking those things without asking but they were important to him and he knew that Grandma would again tell him that he would have to ask his dad. Besides, he told himself, those things belonged to Grandpa Charley, not Grandma.

"Well, Tony, I couldn't find the dog tags. I guess you're out of luck."

"Thanks anyway, Grandma. I really appreciate you looking, but do you mind if I try to find them? I have a few ideas of where they might be."

Tony thought this might give him the opportunity to peruse the house and make sure that he was not missing anything of Grandpa Charley's that he wanted.

"Tony, you've got what you're gonna get. Now be grateful for that."

Tony was a little irritated at Grandma for not letting him look around. However, he was indeed grateful to her for giving him the wallet and coffee mug. He was even more grateful for finding the other items that he had concealed in his pants.

"Grandma, who was Annie?"

His grandmother's already curt attitude turned to anger in an instant.

"What name did you say?"

"Um, Annie?"

"Where did you hear that name? Did you find something with that name on it?"

It was obvious to Tony that he had just asked about someone that he wasn't even supposed to know about, which only piqued his curiosity.

"No, Grandma. I just remember Grandpa Charley saying something about her."

"Don't you lie to me, Tony. What did you find?"

"Grandma, I don't know what you're talking about." Tony decided to push the envelope. "Who was she?"

"She was a mistake and a nobody. Don't you ever mention her name again. Come on. Take me back to your dad's, now."

Tony couldn't imagine his Grandpa Charley cheating on Grandma but maybe he did. Then he realized that the date on the knife was before his grandparents were even married. He had no idea what was going on and he figured that he probably never would. As they arrived back at his dad's house, Hank's wife was sitting on the front porch as if she were waiting for them. Tony got out of the car and opened the door for his grandma. His dad's wife walked up to him and asked him to stay for dinner. Normally, he would have been reluctant to do so but he was actually in a great mood due to the treasures he had received from his grandma's house so he agreed to stay. Besides, he thought it might be his last opportunity to enjoy a meal with his grandma. He also had the added bonus of not having to worry about his dad showing up.

During dinner, Tony's grandma was quiet for the most part. Tony knew that she was still angry about him asking about Annie, not to mention that she wasn't satisfied with how he came to the knowledge of her. On the other hand, Hank's wife never stopped talking. She told Tony that she had talked to his dad on the phone earlier in the day. She asked if he could wait just one more day until his dad could arrive back home so they might have a chance to visit.

"Did Dad actually tell you that he wanted to see me or are you trying to get the two of us together for Grandma?"

His wife did not answer. Tony knew what her lack of a response meant.

"What kind of father doesn't want to see his own child?"

She still didn't say anything.

"If I were to stay, do you think he would give me my rifle back that Grandpa Charley gave me?"

117

She knew exactly which rifle he was talking about. She had been there when he brought it home that summer afternoon.

"Tony, I don't think it would be a good idea for you to ask him for it."

Tony turned back toward Grandma, making it obvious that his conversation with his dad's wife was over.

"It was great to see you, Grandma."

"It was good to see you too, Tony."

"Hey, Grandma, I almost forgot to ask. Where is Grandpa Charley buried?"

"Akins Cemetery, along the main road on the right, just before the first intersection."

"Thanks, Grandma. I love you."

Tony got up from the table, hugged his Grandma and turned to leave. It was obvious that she was still fuming mad. His dad's wife stopped him at the door.

"Tony, just give him a chance. It would mean the world to your grandma if the two of you could at least talk."

Tony knew that she was right. However, it irritated him that she used Grandma to make him feel guilty.

"I tell you what. I'll stay at the motel one more night. If Dad wants to see me, tell him to call me, which is something he's never ever done."

Tony left and went back to the motel. Surprisingly, he had no trouble falling asleep. The next morning he awoke to the sound of the phone ringing.

"Good mornin', Tony."

Tony couldn't believe it. It was his dad. It had been so long since the last time he talked to his dad that he almost didn't recognize his voice.

"I was wondering if you want to come over this morning for pancakes?

"Do you really want to see me or are you calling for Grandma?"

"Why wouldn't I want to see you?"

Tony's experience of his dad was that he never gave a straight answer. *The mind games have started*, Tony thought to himself.

"You've never made any attempt to see me in the past since you dropped me off on June 7th, 1991."

It was the worst day of Tony's life up to that point. He still had not forgiven his dad or his dad's wife for what they did to him that day.

His dad responded in kind. "Tony, you've been gone this long, I guess there's really no reason for you to stop by now."

Tony hung up the phone. He halfway expected the phone to start ringing again. If it did, he had no intention of answering. *He's not worth it*, Tony told himself. However, the phone did not ring again.

CHAPTER 9

Tony checked out of his room and, as planned, wanted to see Grandpa Charley's grave before he left town. He headed to Akins Cemetery. As Tony passed by Flood's feed store, he thought of the good memories there with Grandpa Charley. He always let Tony get a snack when they stopped by for feed. Tony remembered being about nine years old and standing at the counter, pointing to a round can of shredded beef jerky. Tony asked Grandpa Charley if he could get it but he ignored Tony and continued talking to Mr. Flood. It was unusual for Grandpa Charley to ignore him. Tony asked again and Grandpa Charley, again, ignored his plea. Grandpa Charley seemed embarrassed and apologized to Mr. Flood, explaining that Tony didn't really understand what he was asking for. Tony suddenly realized that Grandpa Charley thought it was chewing tobacco like his dad used.

"Grandpa Charley, that ain't chew, it's jerky."

Grandpa Charley had a puzzled look on his face and looked up at Mr. Flood.

"You know, Charley, he's right. It ain't nothin' but jerky."

Grandpa Charley smiled, looking relieved and then laughed.

"Well then, add it to the bill."

Before Tony knew it, he was at the cemetery. He parked just outside the gate and walked in along the dirt road, passing by several headstones until he found Grandpa Charley's. It was strange for Tony to see his own name on a tombstone. He knelt down next to it, realizing that while it had only been a few days since he learned of Grandpa Charley's passing, Grandpa Charley had been in the ground for two months. Tony felt terrible about not being there when his grandfather passed away. He always thought he had more time.

Tony looked around the cemetery to make sure that he was alone and then the tears began to stream down his face as he began speaking to his grandpa as if he were there. "Grandpa Charley, please forgive me. I should have been there for you and I wasn't. If I had only known. I just thought we had more time. I'd give anything to talk to you just one more time."

However, Tony knew that he could never make up for the time he lost. Still yet, he was trying to do all he could now by pouring

121

his heart and soul out to Grandpa Charley but Tony worried that he could not hear him. As a result, he was so focused and in the moment that he lost all sense of time and what was going on around him.

The next time he looked up, he noticed the silhouette of someone standing several feet from him, between him and the afternoon sun. Tony put his hand up to block the sunlight and observed a tall, thin woman wearing a sundress and sunglasses. She had one hand clasping her necklace, the other holding her hair up in an effort to cool the back of her neck from the hot, humid air. She walked up next to him and released her hair. Tony felt somewhat embarrassed because he knew that she caught him having an emotional conversation with Grandpa Charley, who obviously wasn't really there.

Heather was supposed to have already left for Baton Rouge but there was no way she could leave without correcting her missed opportunity the day before to give Grandpa Charley a proper goodbye. As soon as she woke up that morning, she called the moving company to postpone the move for one more day and headed to the cemetery. Upon arriving, she was shocked to find Tony there.

He quickly thought of something to say in order to break the awkward silence, having no idea who she was. "You here visiting a loved one too?"

"Uh huh."

Tony felt even more awkward. He wiped the tears from his face.

"How long have you been standing there?"

"Long enough."

Her voice was soft and soothing. To his surprise, she sat down right next to him so that their knees were touching. She was very beautiful, he thought to himself. Tony didn't know what to say, but somehow he felt the awkwardness begin to dissipate.

"So he was pretty special to you, wasn't he?"

"Yes. He was my grandpa. I wasn't there for him like I should have been and now it's too late."

Tony couldn't believe he was opening up to a complete stranger, but it felt good. Besides, he figured there was no harm in it since he would never see her again.

"Well, why weren't you there for him like you should have been?"

Tony was taken back at her bluntness. She didn't even know him.

"It's a long story. You couldn't really understand without being there."

"Try me."

Again, Tony was caught off guard by her candidness. He was not used to anyone speaking to him so plainly, but again he figured there was no harm in opening up to a stranger.

"Well, as a kid I spent weekends and summers here. I have such great memories of this area."

"And I suppose those weekends and summers were spent with your grandpa?"

"Yes. In fact…" Tony paused and looked around before continuing, "I'm pretty sure that this is the cemetery that me and Grandpa Charley used to pass in the spring on our way to go turkey hunting."

"Turkey hunting? That sounds exciting."

Tony began to relax and enjoy their conversation. *She really seems interested in what I have to say.* His guard was slowly let down and for a moment, he even thought of asking her to dinner after their conversation. But he wasn't in a hurry to rush things. All of a sudden Tony laughed.

"What's so funny?"

"Well, you probably would have to have been there to appreciate it."

"Come on. Give me a chance."

Tony was more than willing to give her a chance. The more he talked to her, the more he wanted to know about her:

"You know, I don't even know your name."

She smiled. "Oh no. You're not getting off that easy. Now what's so funny?"

"Well, on one particular Sunday afternoon, my grandpa and I were returning from a turkey hunt when we ran out of gas about a mile up the road. At first I asked my grandpa what we were going to do but he told me not to worry because 'these things happen for a reason.' My grandpa then told me that he had been waiting for

124

the right time to show me something and as we passed by this cemetery, we came in and walked through it."

Tony remembered the words of Grandpa Charley that day. "This place is not just sacred because the dead rest here, but because there is a young man buried here who touched my life when I was a young boy. The young man did not always do things right, but he did the best he could with what he had."

Tony and Grandpa Charley arrived at the young man's grave. It was a beautiful rose colored tombstone. Grandpa Charley bent down, touched the tombstone and continued. "Tony, you should always give people the benefit of the doubt before judging them. Not everyone is given the same opportunities in life. That was most certainly the case for this young man."

Tony stood up and looked out across the cemetery but he could not remember exactly where the rose colored tombstone was or whose name was on it.

"I figure the man my grandpa told me about must have been famous though because he told me that more than 20,000 people attended that guy's funeral, including himself and his mother."

"That's interesting."

"What do you mean?"

"They say that the infamous outlaw, Pretty Boy Floyd, is buried around here somewhere. In fact, I'm pretty sure his tombstone is right over here."

Heather walked away from Tony and he followed closely behind. He doubted it would be the same tombstone, but at that point he was more interested in Heather than he was in finding the tombstone of a man whose name he didn't think he would recall even if he heard it.

About a hundred yards away from Grandpa Charley's tombstone was a rose-colored tombstone that had been vandalized. All four corners were chipped and a chunk of the tombstone in the middle had been chiseled out, removing most of the "C" from the man's first name.

Tony bent down and read the name aloud, "Charles Arthur Floyd. I don't believe it."

"What don't you believe?"

"You're right. That was the tombstone my grandpa showed me. The strange thing is that my grandpa and that man shared his first and middle names."

Tony stood back up and looked at the woman. She was again clasping her necklace in her hand, slowly running it back and forth along the gold chain.

"So, you still haven't answered my question."

"What question?"

"You said that you weren't there for your grandpa like you should have been. What happened between the two of you?"

Tony really didn't want to go there. He had enjoyed their conversation so far but he wondered why she was so adamant on knowing what happened between him and Grandpa Charley.

"Well, like I said, it would be hard to understand without being there."

"Come on. You've got to give me more than that."

Why, Tony wondered. There was no easy way to explain it. He started to get agitated but then he realized that it wasn't her fault. *She's just inquisitive,* he told himself. Besides, after taking the time to talk to him, he figured the least he could do was attempt to answer her question.

"I'll try to answer your question. You would have to understand that things were very difficult between my father and I and…"

She cut him off before he ever got started. "I know, Number Two. I know. And then you left and never came back and now he's dead. How could you do that to him?"

Heather's patience ran thin. *I knew he was going to use his dad as an excuse,* she told herself. Heather was so angry with him.

Tony's mind began racing. Normally he would have been defensive of such harsh words. However, he had no idea who this woman was. What's more, she had just called him "Number Two," a reference that only Grandpa Charley would have made. Tony tried to remember but he was certain that Grandpa Charley never called him Number Two in front of anyone. It was part of the close bond they shared, a kind of secret code between the two of them. All of a sudden, questions began racing through Tony's mind. *How could she possibly have known that? Who is she? What was she doing there?*

"You still don't even know who I am, do you?"

127

Tony didn't dare answer. The truth was that he had no idea who she was and for the first time during their conversation, he felt as though he should have. This only added to his confusion. His mind was racing and his heart was pounding.

She then reminded him. "You're the only person to ever give me a black eye. Remember? To this day I have never told anyone what really happened because I promised you I wouldn't."

Heather stood up as she raised her voice. "I'm sorry for all that happened to you at the hand of your father but Grandpa Charley deserved more from you. He always believed you'd come back but I never did. You know, his dying wish was that I find a way to contact you but I failed miserably. And now..."

Heather stopped midsentence as Tony reached in his back pocket and pulled out Grandpa Charley's wallet. Tony opened it and flipped through the pictures of the grandkids, pulling out the picture he had seen the evening before. He studied the face of a young girl with sparkling brown eyes and long locks of auburn hair. Tony turned the picture over and again read the back, "Heather, 12 years old."

Is it really her, Tony asked himself. *How is that possible*, he wondered. He knew that her family had moved shortly after he left Sallisaw. And why was she so angry with him? They had been the best of friends.

Heather recognized her picture. She had no idea that Grandpa Charley carried it in his wallet. Tears streamed down her face as she thought of Grandpa Charley and what he had asked her to do.

She agreed to do it because she loved Grandpa Charley but also because she knew that Tony would never come back to Oklahoma, meaning that she would never have to follow through. Yet there he stood. Tony was back and now, more than ever, she felt an obligation to fulfill her promise to Grandpa Charley.

In a way that she couldn't explain, she knew that it had all happened for a reason, just like Grandpa Charley predicted. Yet each time she opened her mouth to talk to Tony, the only thing that came out was anger. *This isn't working. I need some time to pull myself together if there is any way I am going to be able to fulfill Grandpa Charley's wish,* she thought.

"You know what, Tony? Before he died, Grandpa Charley asked me to share some things with you but I don't know that you even care enough to hear it. If by some miracle you do, meet me at Grandpa Charley's favorite restaurant in one hour. That is, if you can even remember where it is."

Heather walked back to her car without saying another word. She worried that she might say something she would regret. Tony watched Heather get in her car before speeding away. Tony walked back over to Grandpa Charley's headstone and placed his hand on it.

"She has a right to be mad, Grandpa Charley. You definitely deserved better than what I gave you. I'm not sure what Heather is doing here or what you have to do with any of this but I plan to find out. Thank you, Grandpa Charley, for everything."

Tony felt like he was on the right track and Grandpa Charley was responsible. He knew exactly where his next stop was. He was headed to Wild Horse Mountain Barbeque.

CHAPTER 10

Tony sat in his car and looked around the parking lot of the restaurant, remembering all of the times he'd been there with Grandpa Charley. The building itself was a wood plank shack on the outskirts of Sallisaw, set back in the woods, which only added to its atmosphere and appeal. The sign was just as worn and faded as it was when Tony was a kid, held in place by two rusty steel poles. As usual, the place was jam packed with cars.

As he sat there, he began to second guess everything he felt at the cemetery. His newly found confidence had seemingly vanished as quickly as it had come. The other voice in his head began to question why he was even there. *After all*, he told himself, *if I were to drive away right now, Heather and I could just go on living our lives as if we had never seen each other again.* But, deep down, Tony knew that wasn't true. Seeing Heather again had changed everything, which was the real reason he felt uneasy. He closed his eyes, took a deep breath and ignored the other voice and chose to heed the much more subtle thoughts telling him to go inside. It was almost as if he could feel his Grandpa Charley pushing him.

Tony walked in and immediately recognized the aroma of smoke and caramelized brown sugar floating on the air. Tony did not immediately see Heather, although she had seen him through the window when he pulled in the parking lot. She wondered when he was finally going to come in. Strangely, Heather found comfort watching him wrestle with his thoughts in the car. After their exchange at the cemetery, she knew that Tony was tormented by his choice to not fill a greater role in Grandpa Charley's life and Heather felt like he deserved it. This knowledge somehow made what she had to tell him easier. However, she was still blown away that she had run into him at the cemetery. *What are the odds?* She asked herself. However, Heather never believed in coincidence. She watched Tony as he looked around the restaurant for her, wishing she were invisible.

When he did not immediately see her, Tony had to consciously ignore the thought that she might not show up. That's when he saw her at the back-corner table, making no attempt to make herself known. Heather forced a smile as Tony walked over and sat down in the booth across from her. She pushed the thought out of her mind that Grandpa Charley probably looked like Tony at that age because if he did, he would have been quite handsome. Tony noticed that Heather had already ordered. There were two specials sitting on the table between them, which included a brisket sandwich, barbeque beans, a pickle and a drink.

"I hope it's still Dr. Pepper?"

"I can't believe you remember that."

"I remember a lot, Tony."

Heather could tell that Tony was unsure of himself. She wondered if there was ever a time in Grandpa Charley's life when he had been unsure of himself and, if so, she wondered where he found his confidence. *Probably the Army*, she told herself. Under normal circumstances, Tony's insecurity might have appealed to her but she just wanted to get this over with. *The sooner, the better*, she thought. Grandpa Charley told her that she would instinctively know what to say when Tony came back yet she didn't have a clue.

"Tony, I'm sorry if what I said at the cemetery seemed harsh, but I meant every word."

"Did I wrong you in some way that I don't remember?"

"It's not me you wronged. You said it yourself. Grandpa Charley deserved more from you. He ached to see you, to know you, to spend time with you. Yet, year after year, you refused to visit him. Let's just get this over with so we can both move on with our lives."

"Get what over with?"

"Grandpa Charley's dying wish was that I tell you who he really was and where he came from. I think he somehow thought that knowledge would help you find yourself. He felt obligated to you, unlike you felt toward him. For some reason, he felt like all of your difficulties in life were somehow his fault. It's obviously going to be uncomfortable for both of us, but a promise is a promise, so let's get on with it."

Tony seemed nervous, which only further irritated her. *What does he have to be nervous about*, she asked herself. After all, she was the one that promised to tell Grandpa Charley's story. He had no obligation to do anything but sit there.

Heather attempted to gather her thoughts but before she could begin, Tony interrupted her. "Heather, what were you doing at the cemetery today?"

At first, Heather refused to answer his question. In an attempt to release some of her frustration, she closed her eyes, took a deep breath and thought through her promise to Grandpa Charley. Everything he had told her, everything she had refused to believe was coming true and she knew that if she was to fulfill Grandpa Charley's request, she had to open up and sincerely share Grandpa Charley's story with Tony. *It's now or never,* she told herself, because come morning light, she was bound for Baton Rouge.

Heather opened her eyes, forced another smile and responded, "Give it a chance, Tony. We'll get there."

Tony had no idea what she meant but noticed that her demeanor had changed. She didn't seem so angry or upset. As the conversation continued, Heather found herself opening up to someone she had considered to be a complete stranger. However, what bothered her most was that now he did not feel like a stranger. Heather began recounting the details of Grandpa Charley's life since childhood, just like he asked her to do.

When Charley was 16 years old, his mother, Lora, passed away suddenly and unexpectedly. At the time Charley believed that the secret of his father's identity had died with her. However, shortly before lying about his age and enlisting in the Army, Charley went through his mother's cedar chest. While Lora didn't have much, he wanted something to remember her by and he knew that whatever wouldn't fit in his suitcase would be lost forever because as far as he was concerned, he was never coming back. In the bottom of the chest, Charley found an old wooden Kraft cheese box containing several love letters, a diamond ring, a semi-automatic Colt pistol, a brass key and two photographs.

The first photo was of a man wearing a fedora, sitting in the driver's seat of a 1929 Ford Model A, with Charley at age 8 on his lap. On the back was written, "Charles and Charley." The second photograph was of Charley's mother standing between Charley and the same man. The back of that photo read, "Charles, Lora and Charley." The letters revealed that Charley's father's name was Charles Floyd. According to the letters, when Charles learned that Lora was pregnant, he bought her an engagement ring and asked her to run away with him. Charley figured that his mother must have refused because in subsequent letters, Charles apologized for not telling her that he was already married and begged Lora to reconsider.

The last letter was dated more than two years before Lora passed way. It was dated October 2, 1934. In it, Charles told Lora that if anything ever happened to him, she was to go to the local barbershop in Sallisaw because the local barber could be "trusted." There was also a newspaper clipping from the Tulsa World dated just 21 days after Charles wrote Lora the last letter. The headline read, 'U.S. Agents Kill Floyd, Phantom Bad Man of Ozarks Falls Before Federal Avengers in Ohio, 14 Slugs in His Back.'

Charley remembered attending the funeral with his mother. It was the only time that she took him on a trip. They travelled to Sallisaw and attended the funeral at Akins Cemetery. Charley had never seen so many people. At the time, Charley did not make the connection that the funeral was for the fancy dressed man who used to visit him, nor did he know the man was his father. Charley wasn't sure why his mother never told him the truth of who his father was but he figured she was either embarrassed about having had a love affair with an outlaw or a married man.

This discovery changed everything for Charley because he wanted to know more about his father. Charley wondered if the barber in Sallisaw was still there. He decided to leave for boot camp early and make a stop in Sallisaw. After all, he wasn't supposed to leave for boot camp for another week. The next morning Charley caught the early morning bus from Cleveland to Tulsa and then from Tulsa to Sallisaw. While it was only 130 miles from Cleveland to Sallisaw, the bus ride took most of the day due to stops and transfers.

Tony interrupted Heather. "I know the rest of this story, Heather. That's where Grandpa Charley met Dewey Padgett at Padgett's Barber Shop. Mr. Padgett let Grandpa Charley stay in the room behind the barber shop and they were friends ever since. Still, it's crazy to believe that Grandpa Charley was the son of Pretty Boy Floyd, that he was my great-grandfather."

Heather reached across the table, took Tony's hands gently in hers and looked him right in the eye. "Tony, there is so much more to the story than you know. Grandpa Charley moving to Sallisaw had nothing to do with the people and everything to do with his father. If you'll let me, I'll tell you the real story of why Grandpa Charley desperately wanted to get back here."

While looking in Tony's eyes Heather had the sudden unintentional thought that he had Grandpa Charley's eyes. She looked away and dismissed the thought as quickly as it entered her mind. Tony felt almost reprimanded but he understood that she was trying to share something that was sacred to her. *It was sacred to him too*, he thought. Tony committed to listen intently to what Heather had to say. He could tell it was difficult for her but he wasn't sure if the difficulty was due to her anger toward him or her love of Grandpa Charley or maybe both.

Heather continued.

The bus dropped Charley off in front of Goodwin's Cafe in Sallisaw at 4:00 p.m. There were several men sitting along the store fronts, as if they had been awaiting the bus' arrival to see who it brought to town. Charley walked down Cherokee Avenue until he saw the barber's pole around the corner on Sequoyah Avenue. He hoped the barber could provide some additional insight into the man his father was.

Charley walked in and met Dewey Padgett for the first time. Dewey was just a few years older than Charley. Charley waited for Dewey to finish giving a haircut to a man already in the barber chair. The man paid and exited the barber shop.

"What'll it be, young man?"

"Sir, my name is Charley Crambrink. I never knew my father but I was told you may have and that I should come see you."

It was obvious that Dewey's curiosity was immediately piqued.

"Oh, yeah? What was your father's name?"

Charley looked around to make sure no one else was around and whispered, "Pretty Boy Floyd."

Dewey laughed.

"That's a name I haven't heard for a while. Around these parts we called him Charles Floyd. The newspapers gave him the nickname Pretty Boy but he hated it. Folks around here will tell you that he was more of a local hero than an outlaw. He may have robbed a few banks but don't believe everything you read. Charles always said the FBI accused him of several murders up in Kansas City that he had nothing to do with in order to elevate his status to public enemy number one."

"So you know the story?"

"You're obviously not from around here. Everyone from these parts knows the stories. Also, no one from around here would be crazy enough to claim to be related to Charles unless it was true. Besides, you're his spittin' image."

"Did you know him personally?"

"Yes. I did know Mr. Floyd. He and my father were close friends. In fact, Mr. Floyd ripped up the mortgage papers for the barber shop and our home when he robbed the bank. It wasn't unusual for Mr. Floyd to destroy specific bank notes and mortgage loans for families in Sequoyah County who assisted him in evading capture over the years. In those days, banks were foreclosing left and right and no one cared how their mortgage was taken care of, especially if it kept them from losing everything. As far as the old timers around here were concerned, Charles Floyd was the Robin Hood of their day."

"Did he ever mention me or my mom?"

"You know, Charley, my family has always known about you. Mr. Floyd told my dad that he had a son named after him with his girlfriend, Lora Crambrink, from Cleveland. However, your mom refused to run away with him when she found out he was already married."

"You don't think it was because he was a wanted man?"

"To hear Mr. Floyd tell it, she didn't care in the least that he was a fugitive. She just didn't want to break up a marriage, especially because he had another son with his wife. I'll tell you one thing though, he never got over your momma. After Mr. Floyd was killed, we never knew what happened to either of you but Mr. Floyd always said that someday you would come looking for him."

Dewey went to the back of his shop and came back with a crowbar. He walked past Charley, locked the front door and turned the sign on the door around, indicating that the shop was closed. At first, Charley was concerned. Dewey must have sensed that he was alarmed because he laughed and told Charley that he had nothing to worry about. Dewey walked to the rear corner of his shop, knelt down and began prying nails up from the floorboards with the crowbar. Charley had no idea what Dewey was up to. He removed several planks and then pulled out a heavy metal bound coffer chest trimmed in heavy brass. It measured eight inches long by four inches wide by four inches tall. The beautiful chest looked almost new. There were spade shaped cutouts in the brass where the wood was exposed. Each wood cutout had either an intricate etching of a large ship with four smoke stacks or a white star. It had a brass lock attached to the front. The top of the chest was engraved with the initials T.C.A.C. and the bottom was stamped, "Made in England." Dewey handed it to Charley.

"Here. Mr. Floyd left this for you. I'm sorry but I don't have the key."

Charley took the box in his arms without saying a word. It was heavier than it looked. He wasn't concerned about a key to open the box because a brass key was among the items he found in the cheese box that belonged to his mother. Charley was sure it would open the coffer chest. He realized that he was now holding the only link between he and his father, and he needed time to think things through.

"Mr. Padgett, do you know where Akins Cemetery is?"

"Of course, and call me Dewey. I'd be happy to take you there."

Dewey instantly knew why Charley wanted to go there. It's where his daddy was buried. They both sat silent during the twenty minutes it took to get to the cemetery outside of town. Charley held the box tightly on his lap and stared out the window. He wondered what secrets the chest held. He had just learned the day before that he was the son of an infamous outlaw shot and killed by the FBI, but now he knew that not everyone saw him as a bandit. It was overwhelming, to say the least. They arrived at the cemetery and Dewey pointed out where Charles Floyd's headstone was.

"I'm going to head just up the road to Flood's Feed Store. You can find me there when you're ready, but feel free to take all the time you need. Say, do you have a place to stay tonight?"

"No, sir."

"No problem. I have a room in the back of my shop. You are welcome to it."

"Thank you for everything, Dewey."

Charley sat down in front of his father's tombstone, the father he had never known. Charley placed his suitcase flat on the ground, opened it and removed the small brass key from his mother's box. He put the key in the lock, turned it and the lock opened with ease. Charley removed the lock and opened the coffer chest to reveal a beautiful purple and gold flowered velvet liner. Inside, there was a

141

picture of Charley at age nine, his mother and Charles. He vaguely remembered taking the photo. At the time, Charley's mother admitted that the man was a relative. After the photo was taken, Charley overheard his mother and Charles yelling at each other. Charles drove away and Charley never saw him again. Charley removed the photo from the coffer chest and found a letter addressed to him.

"Dearest Tony. If you're reading this, I guess by now you know that I wasn't the best father. I know I wasn't there for you like I should have been but it wasn't completely within my control. I loved your mother more than anything and respected her wishes. Please don't blame her. It was my choice to live the life that I did. While there's probably nothin' I could ever do to make up for it, I have left you something but you're gonna have to find it. I'm sorry to have to hide it from you but it was the only way I could ensure that no one else would get it. Carefully follow these instructions:

Follow the old stagecoach line to where it meets up with the Kansas City Southern Railroad. There is an iron bridge that was built by the railroad at the crossing that spans a creek of significant size. Center yourself on the main pillar and walk 222 paces south to a dry well. Turn back west and walk another 1000 paces. You should find two unmarked marble gravestones. If you dig around the base of the gravestones, one of them will have four roman numerals that correspond to letters of the alphabet. Those letters, when deciphered, will spell your initials. Dig down until you find an old handmade coffin. The graves are a decoy. Your *inheritance is inside. It should be enough to ensure that you and your family are taken care of. I'm sincerely sorry that we hadn't known each other better, but just know that the few times I did see you were some of the best moments of my life. Sincerely, Charles Floyd"*

"P.S. Don't ever tell anyone where you got what I left you or the feds will confiscate it."

Charley knew that there wasn't sufficient time to look for what his father had left him before he had to report for boot camp. Yet there was no doubt in his mind that someday he would return to claim what was rightfully his.

CHAPTER 11

A waitress came over to the table and interrupted Heather's story. "Hey, y'all. I don't mean to be a bother but it's 6:00 o'clock and we're closin'."

Tony had not touched his food, which he was a little embarrassed about. But then again, neither had Heather so the waitress wrapped it up for them. Tony had been listening so intently that he had not realized that they were the last two patrons in the restaurant. They walked out to the parking lot and Tony sensed that Heather had something she wanted to ask him but she seemed reluctant.

After walking her to her car, she finally asked, "Tony, if you want to continue our conversation, I guess you can come to my place, but I'm warning you, it's a mess."

Heather wanted to finish her story. Tony had already learned so much about Grandpa Charley that he had never known. He graciously accepted Heather's offer and followed her back to her house. As Heather drove home, her mind was racing. She was thinking about where she had left off and where to pick up. Seeing Tony again was much more difficult than she imagined. It invoked feelings she had not expected, causing something distantly familiar to stir within her. She was still angry with him but as he sat there listening to her story, she was reminded of the friend that she had missed since childhood. She also admitted to herself that, as angry as she was at him for not being at Grandpa Charley's funeral, they probably would not have had the opportunity to talk as openly as they had if Tony had attended the funeral with the rest of the family there. Heather couldn't help but think that Grandpa Charley had somehow planned their meeting. He was the common denominator between them and now his death had brought them back together, exactly as Grandpa Charley had predicted. Heather felt like everything that was happening was part of something larger. Something she couldn't put into words. In fact, Heather knew that if she were to try and explain how she felt to anyone, they would never understand.

Tony had enjoyed seeing Heather. Their reunion was even better than he could have imagined. In Tony's life, true friends were hard to come by and he treasured them. *Heather was no different,* he thought to himself. Yet he asked himself why he hadn't thought about her in years. He supposed that it was because he never expected to see her again. Tony caught himself thinking about how beautiful she was, something he had given no thought to when they were kids. The past few hours had provided the opportunity to reflect on the true friend she had been to him all those years ago. He was surprised to learn that Heather had been living in Sallisaw. She had obviously moved there to be closer to Grandpa Charley, which is why he was not surprised to learn that she was moving away now that he was gone.

Heather pulled into her driveway and Tony parked next to her.

"Well, we're home."

Tony could not have agreed more. He felt at home with her, something that he had rarely felt in his life. Heather invited him in and apologized for the mess. There were boxes everywhere. Heather cleared off the couch and asked him if he needed anything. He asked if she had something cold to drink. She handed him an ice cold can of Dr. Pepper from the refrigerator and offered him a seat on the couch while she freshened up. Tony sat down and enjoyed his favorite soda. He looked around the room at the bare walls and focused his eyes on a photograph sitting on the mantle that he had never before seen. However, he remembered the event.

Tony got up and walked over to the fireplace. He picked the picture up and carefully studied it. It was a picture of Grandpa Charley, Heather, and himself the last summer they were together, riding Grandpa Charley's horses in the Sallisaw Rodeo parade. There was also a newspaper clipping laying in the corner of the frame, partially covering up the photo. It was Grandpa Charley's obituary. As Tony read it for the first time, tears welled up in his eyes.

"Memorial Obituary: Tony Charles Arthur Crambrink, 89, of Sallisaw died Thursday, June 13, 2009, in Sallisaw. He was born October 6th, 1920, in Cleveland, Oklahoma. He was a United States Army veteran of World War II, a farmer and rancher, former manager and L.P. Gas man for Farmers Co-op in Sallisaw, a member of American Legion in Ft. Smith, a 32nd degree Mason, a member of Lodge No. 205 in Cleveland, Oklahoma, and a Baptist."

As Tony finished reading his Grandpa Charley's obituary, he realized that Heather was standing next to him. She put her arms around him and gave him the sweetest hug he had ever felt. *She really gets me the way Grandpa Charley did*, he thought to himself.

"I've missed you, Heather. I'm so sorry for everything."

Heather did not speak. She wasn't sure she wanted to go down that path. She walked away and began digging through a couple of boxes until she found the two scented candles that she was looking for. However, she couldn't find any matches. Tony smiled and took the candles from her, clearly content with himself that he had thought of something she hadn't.

He walked over to the kitchen, lit the candles on the stove and placed the candles on the coffee table. Heather turned off the lights. They sat next to each other on the floor with only the light of the candles on their faces. For a fleeting moment, Tony felt as if their perfect childhood friendship had never faded. In that brief moment, Heather too, felt like her long-lost friend had returned and she was grateful to Grandpa Charley for bringing them back together.

Tony noticed a large manila envelope sitting on the coffee table next to them. Heather must have laid it there at some point, because he was sure that it had not been there before.

"What's that?"

Without saying a word, Heather reached over, picked up the envelope and pulled an old yellowed piece of paper from it. It was the original letter Grandpa Charley's father wrote to him. The same letter that Grandpa Charley found in the coffer chest.

"I suppose the coffer chest has been lost to time but Grandpa Charley gave me the letter that he found inside. He wanted you to have it."

"Wow. Do you think Grandpa Charley ever found whatever Charles Floyd left for him?"

"Well, according to Mr. Flood, he did."

Heather went on to tell Tony about her experience with Mr. Flood and the information that he had shared with her.

"Did Mr. Flood say what Grandpa Charley did with the rest of the money?"

"Mr. Flood never actually saw what was in the canvas bag."

"Well, if Grandpa Charley paid off his mortgage, there must have been something of value in the bag."

"I agree, but no one, including Mr. Flood, really knows. But one thing is for certain, Grandpa Charley predicted all of this."

"How do you think he could have known?"

"He knew a lot, Tony. You would have known that if you had been around more."

Tony lowered his head. *She's right,* he thought to himself. His grandpa had known a lot. A lot more than Tony ever gave him credit for. Tony ached for a way to redeem himself but with Grandpa Charley gone, he knew that was no longer a possibility and he knew that Heather knew it too. Even so, Tony could not have imagined that night turning out any better. He had no idea what time it was but he knew that it was time for him to go, especially if he was going to get any sleep before the long drive back to Houston the following day. He also knew that Heather was headed to Baton Rouge in the morning.

Heather felt a real sense of accomplishment. She knew that Grandpa Charley would have been proud of her for sharing her thoughts and feelings. She didn't know why it surprised her that Grandpa Charley had been right, but Tony already seemed better off with his newly found knowledge of his past and where he had come from. Tony stood up and Heather quickly followed. He then hugged her.

"Thank you, Heather, for everything. This is a day I will never forget."

Tony walked toward the door and pulled the keys from his pocket. Heather followed to show him out. While Tony had an overwhelming desire to stay, he knew that he had already overstayed his welcome. Tony grabbed the door knob just before Heather turned in the opposite direction.

"Tony, wait. I can't believe I almost forgot. We're not done yet."

Heather ran to another room and quickly returned with another envelope in her hand. Tony had no idea what it was, but in that moment he didn't care. He was grateful to stay a little while longer. He slipped the keys back into his pocket.

"Grandpa Charley left this for you."

"What is it?"

"It's a letter from Grandpa Charley. I picked it up from his attorney when I got my letter but I never dreamed I would ever have the chance to give it to you."

Heather handed it to him.

"You are welcome to open it here or take it with you. I could always step into the other room if you want to take the time to read it now."

Tony didn't think twice.

"There's no reason for you to go anywhere. I'd like to open it with you if you're OK with that."

Heather put her hand on Tony's arm.

"I'd love that."

They walked back into the living room and Heather turned the light on before sitting on the couch next to Tony. Tony handed the letter back to Heather.

"You read it. I'm too nervous."

Heather reluctantly took the envelope, wondering what Grandpa Charley had to say to Tony.

"Are you sure?"

Tony nodded. He was anxious to hear what Grandpa Charley's last words to him were. But more than that, he was grateful to Grandpa Charley for giving him the excuse to spend a little more time with Heather. She slid her fingernail under the flap of the envelope and tore it open. There was a single sheet of paper inside, folded into thirds. Heather removed the paper and began reading:

"Dearest Number Two,

If you are reading this, then this old confederate can almost rest in peace. I know life has been difficult for you, my boy, but you have to learn to forgive yourself if you're ever going to find the happiness you deserve. It's closer than you think and well within your grasp. I know you have a lot of questions, and if Heather found you, and I suspect if you're reading this then she did, you already know more about me than you ever knew when I was alive.

However, there's a bit more to learn. You may ask yourself why I went to all the trouble to arrange things the way I have, but it was necessary, and it's what my father would have done. In writing this letter, I now understand why my father led me down a difficult path to give me what he left for me. It was the same reason that I do that for you now. To protect you and Heather from those that would do you harm, from those that would desire to have what

151

*is rightfully yours. Please don't give up before you reach the end
of your journey.*

*It will take both of you, together, to complete the next step. This
means neither of you will be able to do it or understand the clues
alone, which is by design. As reluctant as you may be, due to
feelings you may have or other obligations in your life, this journey
is more important than anything else. In the letter he left for me,
my father told me the same thing. I only wish that I had heeded his
advice long before I did. If I had, it would have changed my life a
lot sooner than it did.*

*Listen to me, despite the difficulty and fear you face at the
prospect of moving forward. It will lead you both back to the
beginning and all of your dreams will come true in ways you could
never have imagined possible.*

*First, go to the place where you both used to bury hidden
treasure. There, you will find the key to your past and future."*

Tony turned to Heather.

"You don't think?"

"I don't know what to think."

This was a complete shock to both of them. While neither Tony
nor Heather understood exactly what Grandpa Charley was up to,
they both knew exactly where he wanted them to go. There was a
large hickory tree in the middle of Grandpa Charley's farm near
the Big Pond. When they were 11 years old, the tree was struck by
lightning on July 4th. As a result, the stump was burned and
hollowed out well below the surface of the ground. Grandpa

Charley had given them a green military ammunition can that they hid inside the stump. As kids, they placed things inside that were important to each of them. Tony put his favorite fishing lure inside that Grandpa Charley gave him, a Heddon Lucky 13. Heather kept a picture of her daddy and his ball cap inside.

Tony was excited and wanted to leave immediately. Heather, on the other hand, was apprehensive about going onto Patty's property, especially in the middle of the night. Tony attempted to convince Heather that even if his grandma did catch them, she would be irritated but wouldn't do anything drastic because Tony was there. Besides, Tony told her, Grandma was living with his dad. Heather relented, which didn't take too much convincing since she really wanted to find out what Grandpa Charley had placed inside. Strangely, she also wasn't ready to let Tony leave.

"Tony, I tell you what. I'm game if you drive."

"Well, what are we waiting for? Let's go."

They stopped by Wal-Mart and picked up a shovel and a couple of flashlights. On the way to the farm Tony wondered how Grandpa Charley knew about the tree stump. As far as he knew, no one knew of its existence except for himself and Heather. He figured that Heather must have shown Grandpa Charley at some point, even though they made a pact to never divulge the secrets of the stump to anyone else.

"When was the last time you looked inside the ammo can?"

"Tony, I promised you that I would never take the can out of the stump without you there and I never have. The last time I saw it was with you."

"Then how do you think Grandpa Charley knew about it?"

"I never told him about it when we were kids. It was our secret."

Heather paused for a moment before continuing.

"But a couple of years ago, while walking the fence line to see where a calf had gotten out, Grandpa Charley and I came to the stump. He mentioned removing it with the tractor. I may have become a bit emotional at the thought of disturbing the stump, as you can imagine, and I told Grandpa Charley that I missed you. Grandpa Charley told me that he missed you too."

A flood of feelings hit Tony. He knew he should have been there walking the fence line with them but life had not afforded him that opportunity. Partially due to circumstances out of his control and partly due to his own choices, which he knew he was accountable for.

Heather continued, "I told Grandpa Charley that when we were kids the stump had been a special place for us that we promised to only visit together and that, as far as I knew, we still had hidden treasures inside. Grandpa Charley told me to always keep that promise and I have. When Grandpa Charley was in the hospital, he reminded me of that conversation. He told me that you also had hidden treasures inside you, just like the stump, but that like our treasure box, they were locked deep inside. He then told me that I was the only one with the combination to unlock those treasures. At the time, I didn't believe Grandpa Charley."

Tony felt the pit of his stomach tighten. He knew what question he wanted to ask next but he was afraid of the answer. *What do I have to lose,* he asked himself. Tony surprised himself as the words left his mouth, "So do you believe Grandpa Charley now?"

Heather looked at Tony, knowing that he was trying to feel her out. He felt her looking at him but he never took his eyes off the road.

"It's not so much that I don't believe him, I just don't know how I would ever accomplish that."

Tony asked himself what all of this meant. Heather also thought back on the events of the day. She realized that everything that had happened had led her to this moment, here with Tony. They parked the car in Grandpa Charley's driveway, next to the house. Tony got the shovel and flashlights out of the trunk.

As they headed out into the pasture, Tony was trying to figure out how to break the silence but Heather beat him to the punch. "Are you going to get the gate or just stand there?"

"Sorry, just thinking about things. It's a lot to take in."

Heather laughed because she knew that Tony was trying to figure out what to say to her.

"I know. It really is. I still can't believe that you're here."

"To tell you the truth, me neither."

Tony stepped forward and opened the gate, shutting it behind them. They walked down the same path that they had walked so many times as children. It took them by the Old Pond, the woods and the fire ant piles that they used to burn with a magnifying glass. As they approached the Big Pond, Tony stopped before going through the open gate. Heather wasn't sure what he was waiting for.

"Is everything OK?"

"I'm just remembering this place. Some of my best memories are here."

Heather took him by the hand and gently pulled him through the gate.

"Come on, Tony."

They stepped through and observed the old hickory stump just inside the gate. It had been out in plain sight all those years yet only three people in the world knew the secrets it contained. Heather turned the flashlight on and shined it into the old stump. It surprised them to see that over the years it had filled up nearly halfway with dirt and was full of weeds. Heather handed the shovel to Tony and smiled.

"Do you mind?"

"Not at all."

The anticipation of what lay beneath the surface excited them both. Tony dug down about six inches but didn't find anything. Heather encouraged him to keep going. She knew that Grandpa Charley would not have mentioned it in his letter if there were nothing there. Tony dug another several inches, until finally the shovel struck metal. They looked at each other, their eyes wide.

Tony dug around the edges and pulled the old ammo can out. It was no longer green as the paint had long since faded and surface rust had taken its place. The combination padlock had been cut, which was a good thing because neither of them remembered the combination.

They looked at each other again and Tony exclaimed, "Grandpa Charley."

Tony pulled the broken lock from the can and opened it. Inside lay the treasures they had enjoyed as children. Tony's fishing lure and Heather's daddy's picture and hat. Heather shined the light on her daddy's face, wondering what life would be like if he were still around. Tony shined his light back into the ammo can and noticed something that they had not placed in the box. It was another large envelope, similar to the one that Heather had laid on her coffee table earlier that evening. Tony pulled the envelope from the can.

"What do you think this is?"

"I'm not sure but it has Grandpa Charley's name all over it. Open it."

Tony opened the envelope. There were two folded letters from Grandpa Charley. One with Heather's name on it and one that said, "Number Two." Heather sat down on the ground and held her letter close to her heart, together with the hat and photograph.

Tony shined the flashlight across his letter and unfolded it. The upper right corner said Sallisaw, OK. Under that was the date, "June 25, 2007." The letter read:

157

"Dearest Tony, if you are reading this, I know you are together with Heather, which makes my heart proud. Take care of her. She's been through more than you know. Under no circumstances do I want you to share this letter with her, nor do I want her to share her letter with you, at least not yet.

I walked this fence line with Heather two days ago when she told me about this stump and the treasures in it. I had no idea you kids hid that ammo can in the old stump but I was sure glad you did. It provided the necessary means for me to accomplish the task at hand. Number Two, I see a lot of you in that old stump. The years of hurt have hardened your bark on the outside but inside you are as soft and tender as the fertile soil. Like the stump, you also hold hidden treasures. Did you find the stone in the bottom of the ammo can? Do not lose it! It is the key and you will need it to unlock your future. As soon as Heather has figured out her piece of the puzzle, she will have something to share with you. Only then will each of you, together, be able to unlock your destiny. Preparation will qualify you. Tony, do not make the same mistake I made. I love you, my boy, and always have. Old Number One will be waiting on Number Two."

Tony shined his light back into the ammo can. He saw a rose-colored stone down in the bottom corner. He reached in and pulled it out, instantly recognizing that it had been chipped off a tombstone. It was smooth on one side and rough on the other with a partial letter "F" carved on the smooth side. The rough side appeared to have a hole drilled in it that had been filled in with some sort of resin or epoxy.

Tony looked over at Heather as she was silently reading her letter:

"Heather, I know from our conversations that you see the hidden treasures in Number Two as I do. Your old granddad is 87 years young and I have learned my way around this old world. Do you remember Sarge? He was my dog, if you can call him a dog. He was 10% dog and 90% wolf. When you went to check the cows if there was a sick one, he notified you. If you pulled a calf, his job was to clean the calf's nose holes so the calf could breath. Sarge always did his job perfect and he was the best helper and friend I ever had, until the two of you came along. Circumstances did not always allow us to be together but I know that the four of us, including Sarge (ha ha), had a special bond that can never be broken. Now Sarge and I have left this old world and you have once again found each other. Where you go from here is up to you. Sarge and I will be looking in on you from time to time and waiting for the day when we all see each other again.

It will take you some time to figure it out but, at the end of this letter, I am leaving you a secret code that you need to figure out. Being the writer that you are, I don't expect it will take you too long to decipher. This is your old Number One signing off.

Love, Grandpa Charley.

P.S. The code is 509-II XXI V XIV I-XXII IX XIX XX I-I XXII V XIV XXI V-XIX I XIV-XII XXI IX XIX-XV II IX XIX XVI XV-III I-

93405. Heather, don't make the same mistake I did or you will regret it forever."

Heather wasn't the least bit worried about Grandpa Charley's secret code. She already knew the cipher. It was the same format that Grandpa Charley's father had left him on the old tombstone near the ghost bridge. Of course, had Mr. Flood not already shared that information with her it would have taken much more time for her to figure out.

Both Tony and Heather were completely overwhelmed. Grandpa Charley had just spoken to both of them from beyond the grave, which neither of them had expected. They carefully placed their treasures back inside the ammo can, placed the broken lock back on the can and put it safely back inside the stump before covering it back up. They left the property undetected just as daylight began to appear in the eastern sky. They were exhausted. Heather quickly fell asleep as Tony drove back to Heather's house. He softly woke her after arriving and she apologized for dozing off. They walked back in the house and Heather immediately went to the kitchen. Tony followed.

"Tony, would you mind placing those two boxes on the floor?"

"Sure thing."

Tony could tell that Heather was up to something.

"What are you doing?"

"You said that Grandpa Charley asked us not to share our letters with each other but he didn't say we couldn't discuss them. Agreed?"

Tony nodded.

"Does your letter contain a code of any kind?"

"I don't think so. What do you mean?"

Heather laughed.

"Why does Grandpa Charley tell you everything and expect me to figure out his little secret codes?"

"I guess he figured you are smarter than me."

They both laughed. Heather got a piece of paper and a pen and began writing.

"509 Buena Vista Avenue, San Luis Obispo, CA 93405"

It's an address, Heather thought to herself. *What would be there,* she wondered, *and why did Grandpa Charley want her to go all the way to California to find out?* This whole thing just got much more complicated. *What was Grandpa Charley really trying to accomplish?* Heather wondered.

Tony stood next to her watching intently as she worked out the coded message. She smiled in satisfaction and leaned in to show him that she had solved the code. When she looked up in his direction, he leaned in and gently kissed her. At first Heather placed her hand on Tony's sculpted chest and also leaned in. Then, a feeling of disloyalty rushed through her. She felt as if she were betraying Grandpa Charley. This was the same guy who never came back to the farm and now she was kissing him? Heather quickly pushed him away and a tear ran down her cheek.

"I can't."

There was a sudden knock at the door.

161

"The movers."

Heather quickly walked away from Tony and headed toward the door, grateful that they had provided her the opportunity to walk away. She let the movers in while Tony stayed in the kitchen and waited for her to return.

"Is there anything more you want to discuss?"

Heather knew exactly what he was talking about. *We don't even really know each other,* she thought to herself. They had shared an intimate, vulnerable moment but it was over. And as far as Heather was concerned, it had been a mistake.

"Tony, we both know how this ends. I mean, the past 24 hours have been wonderful but we were both just caught up in the moment. You have your life to get back to and I'm on my way to Baton Rouge." As she said this, she saw hurt and disappointment flash across Tony's face, but he also knew she was right. There was nothing more to discuss. It was time they went their separate ways.

Tony understood what Heather was trying to say. He cleared his throat and said, "You're right, I also need to get going and fly back to Houston."

Heather was satisfied that she had accomplished the expectations Grandpa Charley had of her with regard to Tony, but there was definitely a part of her that was sad to see him go.

"It was great to see you again, Tony."

"Thanks for everything, Heather."

They awkwardly shook hands. Then Tony left for Houston and Heather headed toward her new life in Louisiana.

CHAPTER 12

The long drive gave Heather plenty of time to think. She was disappointed that she was not more excited about moving forward with her life. But she knew why. It was the combination of the unknown address that Grandpa Charley left her and the way things had ended with Tony. He had kissed her and she knew that she hadn't handled it well. *What did he expect,* she asked herself. Heather rarely had difficulty organizing her thoughts but she had a difficult time making sense of everything that had happened in the last 24 hours. In an effort to soothe her troubled mind, Heather tried to think about anything else. Heather thought about her classes at LSU that were scheduled to begin in two weeks. She would be starting office hours a week from tomorrow and she wondered if any students would stop by her office before classes began. *I doubt it,* she told herself.

Without realizing it, the thought of the mystery address in California crept back into her mind. She wondered if she had decoded the message correctly, but she was sure that she had. She stopped for gas and got a bite to eat. Before getting back on the highway, Heather looked up the address on her phone. It was a residence relatively close to the beach. None of it made sense to her. *What does some random house near the beach have to do with Grandpa Charley,* she wondered. She reminded herself that nothing regarding Grandpa Charley was random. Per Grandpa Charley's instructions, she had not read Tony's letter but she saw him remove a golf ball sized red stone from the ammo box. She wondered what it was but she didn't ask. It was all so cryptic. *Why didn't Grandpa Charley just tell them what they needed to know,* she asked herself. While she didn't like it, Heather knew the answer. Grandpa Charley was much more complicated than that.

After 10 hours of driving, Heather pulled in to her new apartment complex and walked into the empty apartment. It was exactly as she imagined. *It really is perfect,* she thought. However, the movers still wouldn't be there for at least two more days. The last thing Heather wanted to do was sit around an empty apartment consumed by her thoughts. She couldn't help herself. Heather looked up the driving directions to San Luis Obispo, California on her phone. It was 2,003 miles each way. There was no way she had the time or desire to drive that far. She knew airfare would be too high, especially with such short notice, but she looked anyway.

Heather was shocked. A flight from New Orleans to Los Angeles was only $290 if she left the next day and returned Saturday, just in time to begin her new job on Monday. All of a sudden the possibility of going to California was not only real but Heather was now confronted with how committed she was to Grandpa Charley's cause. Before she had the opportunity to talk herself out of it, Heather purchased the ticket. She wondered if going to California was just an excuse to avoid visiting her daddy's plantation but quickly dismissed the thought. It didn't matter because regardless, she was on her way to California. She didn't even have to pack her suitcase because it was already packed.

Heather arrived at LAX at 8:50 a.m. It was an easy non-stop flight. She rented a car and headed up the Pacific Coast Highway. Within a few short hours, Heather arrived in San Luis Obispo and parked down the street from the residence. It was not quite as close to the beach as it appeared on the map. She got out of the car and walked toward it. Heather could see the house in the distance. She recognized it from the street view she had seen the day before on her phone. As she got closer, Heather stared at the house wondering what she was supposed to do there. It was white with a large front porch. The yard was meticulously manicured and a porch swing hung from the porch's ceiling. Heather walked up the concrete walkway and knocked on the screen door. A lovely older woman answered the door.

"Can I help you?"

"I'm not sure. The truth is... well, I'm not sure what I'm doing here or if I'm even in the right place."

The woman came out of the house onto the front porch.

"Maybe I can help you. What's the address you are looking for?"

"Um, I think it's yours."

"Do you know the name of the person you're looking for?"

"Not exactly. It's hard to explain. My grandpa left me a letter with this address but no other details."

The woman's face changed. At first, she looked completely distressed and her chin began to quiver. *This is getting awkward,* Heather thought to herself.

"Was your grandpa from Oklahoma?"

"Yes, ma'am."

The woman sat down on the steps, dropped her face in her lap and wept. After several minutes she responded, "Heather, I'm sorry. It's just that I have missed him so much throughout my life. He's gone, isn't he?"

Heather was confused. She had to be in the right place. *How else would the woman have known her name,* she wondered. Heather thought of how Tony must have felt when she called him Number Two at the cemetery before he realized who she was. Heather sat down next to the woman and put her arm around her.

"Yes, ma'am. He passed away in June. You see, he left me this letter with a coded message. When I decoded it, it was your address."

The woman wiped her tears. Heather wanted to ask her who she was but thought it better to wait while the woman mourned the loss of Grandpa Charley. He had never mentioned her before, yet for some reason he had sent Heather there. The woman stood up and walked back toward the front door.

"Come on in. You must have a hundred questions."

Heather followed her inside. Her house was immaculate. Hardwood floors ran throughout the home, pictures hung from one end of the hallway to the other like a collage of the past to the present, and a fresh bouquet of flowers adorned the entryway table. It was simple yet elegant. The woman told Heather to have a seat on the couch in the front room and she would return shortly. End tables were perfectly placed on either side of the couch with potted plants in ornate clay pots that rested on top of each end table. Three of the walls were painted light blue with white trim that reminded Heather of the ocean. However, the entire fourth wall was covered by a huge photo of a beautiful beach scene. There was a rough and jagged rock face leading to a tall cliff, with a large cave at the bottom. The beach was laden with golden sand with a couple of large rocks poking up out of the sand near the rock face with a pier in the distance. The sea was greenish-blue as the waves rushed in and several seagulls floated, as if weightless, on the sea breeze. Heather had been so mesmerized by the beauty of the scenery on the wall that she hadn't noticed the woman come back into the room.

"It's beautiful, isn't it?"

"It's gorgeous. Where is it?"

"That's the northern most part of Pismo Beach. Charley took me there when we were dating. I'm sorry for before. It's just that when I realized who you were, I knew he was gone, and as long as I have known this day was coming, I knew I would never be prepared."

Heather sat quietly, wanting to know more. It was obvious that the woman loved Grandpa Charley. She offered Heather a cold glass of freshly squeezed raspberry lemonade. She then walked over to a built-in corner cabinet and removed a small wooden chest from it. The woman walked back over to the couch and sat next to Heather, placing the chest on her lap. Because of the way she grasped it with both hands, Heather could tell that it was important to her. The chest was unmistakable. She recognized it from Grandpa Charley's description of the coffer chest that his father had left for him at Padgett's Barber Shop.

"Is that Grandpa Charley's coffer chest?"

The woman was surprised that Heather knew about the chest.

"How do you know about his coffer chest?"

"The night Grandpa Charley died, he told me several things that I had never known, but…"

Heather stopped herself. She was going to tell the woman that he had never mentioned her but she stopped herself for fear that it might hurt the woman's feelings.

"He never told you about me, did he?"

Heather shook her head no, feeling sorry for the woman.

"It's OK. We never told anyone about each other after we married other people and moved on with our lives. In fact, to protect those we love, we kept our distance over the years and were careful not to cross any lines that could be misconstrued as cheating in any sense of the word."

Heather attempted to listen but was completely distracted by the possibility of what could have been inside the coffer chest. Heather knew that if Grandpa Charley had given the chest to the woman, she had to be important to him. The woman sensed Heather's curiosity as Heather's eyes kept wandering back toward the chest.

"I know you are wondering who I am and how I knew Charley. Let's just start from the beginning with a proper introduction. My name is Anne Eleace but your grandpa called me Annie. I have loved him all my life."

Annie pulled her necklace out from inside her shirt and a small brass key hung on it, which she used to open the lock on the chest. Annie opened the lid and removed an object, careful to keep it concealed, and then closed the chest. She reached out toward Heather to place the object in Heather's hand.

"There's no doubt that Number Two has been looking for these."

Annie dropped Grandpa Charley's dog tags into Heather's hands. Heather was amazed.

"How did you get these? Tony used to wear them when we were kids."

Annie paused and stared out the window. A tear ran down her cheek until it landed on her lips. Still staring out the window, she answered, "Charley left me with enough memories to last a lifetime. But even still, our time was cut way too short. Heather, I will tell you things that I have yearned to say out loud for so many years but have never uttered to another soul. I will do that because it was the last wish of a man I loved with all my heart. I have missed him so much."

Annie looked at Heather, her eyes still wet from tears, and grabbed Heather's hands.

"Heather, if you will indulge an old woman, I'll tell you so much more than how I got his dog tags. I will tell you Charley's legacy."

Heather didn't utter a sound and Annie continued. "Let me start from the beginning…"

CHAPTER 13

The first six years in the military went by quickly for Charley. After being among the first combat troops sent to Europe during World War II earlier in the year, he had been promoted again and was now one of the youngest Master Sergeants in the Army. The onset of war had caused the Army to significantly increase their number of recruits to boost the number of soldiers fighting in Europe. This also caused several of those already fighting in Europe to return to the United States to train and lead the large number of new recruits due to their combat experience. As a result, in April of 1942, Charley received orders to go to Chicago to take command of a platoon of Military Police Officers. Charley loved serving in the Army. He considered himself a "company man" and had every intention of retiring from the Army after completing his 20 years. Growing up in Cleveland, Oklahoma he was a nobody who had been ridiculed for being the illegitimate son of a single mother. But in the Army he felt like he mattered and he never took that for granted. Charley had developed a reputation for following orders and getting the job done, no matter the cost, which was the reason he had been promoted so quickly.

Within days of being assigned to Chicago, Charley received new orders reassigning him to a much smaller prison encampment for American citizens of Japanese descent in Tulare, California. Charley immediately filed a request to remain in Chicago. He was already in command of a much larger unit than he would be in Tulare, which he knew would provide a faster means of promotion to the rank of First Sergeant, the highest rank an enlisted soldier could achieve. As a First Sergeant, Charley would be assigned to run the day-to-day operations of an entire base, under the command of the assigned General.

Normally, when new orders were issued, like the ones assigning Charley to Tulare, there was no changing them. However, Charley's stellar military record and rank could not be ignored. As a result, he was afforded the option to stay in Chicago rather than being reassigned to Tulare. Yet his commanding officer made it clear that if he made the decision to stay in Chicago he would lose his promotion to Master Sergeant because the Colonel in Tulare had specifically requested Charley by name. Charley questioned who this Colonel was and what his motives were for requesting him personally, which made him suspicious from the beginning. However, Charley realized that he had no choice if he wanted to maintain his rank. *I guess I'm on my way to California,* he thought to himself.

After arriving in Tulare, Charley was surprised at the large number of civilians in the area that were from Oklahoma, which included a young farm girl named Addlene Attaway. Her friends and family called her Patty. Like so many other Okies in the 1930s, Patty's family moved to Tulare to work at Tagus Ranch after being forced to leave their farm in Oklahoma due to the Dust Bowl. The Dust Bowl was what they named the severe drought with sustained high winds that blew all of the top soil away, making it impossible to grow crops or graze cattle.

Once Patty's family arrived in Tulare, they quickly learned that the work was more that of an indentured servant than a free laborer. All migrant farm workers were required to live on the ranch in wooden shacks. The exorbitant cost of the substandard housing was subtracted from their pay and the remainder of their meager wages was paid in "Tagus money," which was only good at the Tagus Store. This made it impossible for migrant families to save money and move back to Oklahoma, which most of them had planned from the start when they left their homes.

From the time Patty turned 12 years old, she was required to pick fruit with her siblings and parents after school, weekends and summers until she completed the eighth grade. After that, her parents made her quit school to work full time in order to pay her own cost to the family. Like her parents, Patty worked between 12 and 16 hours a day, six and sometimes seven days per week. For the first several years, Patty felt enslaved by the work, knowing that she would never be able to save any real money to leave the ranch. However, all of that changed when the federal government identified Tulare as the site for a new prison encampment called the Assembly Center.

While the Assembly Center falsely and sadly imprisoned nearly 5,000 American citizens of Japanese descent solely on the basis of race and heritage, it became a great symbol of hope for Patty and many other destitute young women looking for an escape. It provided them with over 100 new soldiers who were willing to take the desperate young women out for a night on the town. However, for those women lucky enough to marry a soldier, it was like winning the lottery. As a result of their desperation, the soldiers took full advantage of the plentitude of young women willing to indulge in their every desire.

Patty was no different. She realized early on that if she was to be one of the lucky few to escape Tagus Ranch, she had to do whatever was necessary. Patty became exceptionally skilled at becoming whoever the soldier wanted her to be, which made her feel needed and wanted, two sentiments Patty had never experienced before the soldiers arrived. She was more successful with some than others but if Patty really liked her date, and there had been several that she had liked, Patty let them take her home. Of course, this meant slipping into the window of her bedroom before dawn, careful not to wake her siblings, so that she could get ready for work. However, recently she met a handsome young Lieutenant named Leno Jorgensen and she thought just maybe he was the one that might take her away from Tulare.

Leno had just begun his career in the Army right out of college and had been assigned as the Camp Director of the Assembly Center, under the direction of the Colonel. Normally, this responsibility would have fallen to the First Sergeant of the unit. However, the Assembly Center was small enough that no First Sergeant had been assigned. When Leno met Patty, he was not looking for a serious relationship, and being new to the Army, he was not yet wise to the motives of the women of a military town. As far as Leno was concerned, Patty was unlike any woman he had ever known and he was crazy about her. He thought that she was pretty, spontaneous and above all, fun. At least that is who she pretended to be with him.

Patty didn't much care for Leno. Patty felt that for an educated, commissioned officer, Leno was entitled and immature. But the one thing she loved about dating him was his rank and responsibility. Every time they went out, which had become often, Patty felt like all eyes were on her because she was the Camp Director's girlfriend. Almost like a drug, the attention was addicting and Patty loved it.

One particular Friday evening, Leno took Patty to Tad's Drive-In on Mooney Boulevard in the nearby town of Visalia. It was Patty's favorite place to eat. They had the best burgers around and

Patty loved listening to music from the jukebox. As Leno and Patty sat in their usual booth, she noticed a dashing soldier in uniform walk into the restaurant by himself. She had never seen him before but he had more stripes on his sleeve and medals on his chest than any other soldier she had seen. Needless to say, she was thoroughly impressed. Careful not to seem over eager for fear of making Leno jealous, she leaned over and quietly asked him who the soldier was.

Leno looked toward the door, rolled his eyes and answered, "That's Master Sergeant Crambrink. He's the Colonel's new pet."

"What does that mean?"

"It means that the Colonel requested him personally. I think they must know each other but the Colonel hasn't said anything about him other than when he had me fill out the request to have Sergeant Crambrink transferred here."

"What are all those medals for?"

"All that means is that he has kissed up to whoever he needed to in order to get promoted because he is way too young to be a Master Sergeant."

Patty could relate, she thought to herself. That is exactly how she felt with Leno and all of the other soldiers she had dated. She was quite literally "kissing up" to them to get "promoted" out of Tulare. To say the least, she was intrigued by the new Master Sergeant and she wanted to know more about him.

Leno continued, "I'm sure that he thinks he is going to be promoted to the rank of First Sergeant, which would make him the

Camp Director over me. But I don't care if he knows the Colonel or not, that's not going to happen as long as I have anything to say about it."

It was the first time Patty had seen Leno feel threatened by another soldier. Patty had been dating soldiers long enough to understand military rank, and she knew that as an officer, Leno technically outranked all enlisted soldiers, including Sergeant Crambrink. However, she also knew that Sergeant Crambrink's years of service, medals and rank, would instantly have the respect and admiration of any soldier, something Leno lacked due to his inexperience and sense of entitlement. Leno was becoming disenchanted with Patty's continued interest in Sergeant Crambrink.

"Don't worry, Patty. Sergeant Crambrink won't be spending any time with us. He thinks he's too good to enjoy a night on the town with the rest of us."

"Why do you say that?"

Leno explained that shortly after Charley's arrival in Tulare, Leno had invited him out for drinks, which was customary when a new soldier arrived. However, Charley refused. When Leno asked why he didn't want to go out with the other soldiers, Charley responded, "Would you rather be in a room full of soldiers or be the only soldier in the room?"

Charley knew from their initial meeting that Leno demanded respect solely on the basis of his rank but as far as Charley was concerned, he hadn't earned it. Charley's answer completely offended Leno. As an officer, he felt like no enlisted soldier should ever turn down any request he made, regardless of rank. Charley knew that Leno had a lot to learn about military customs and respect.

Patty's initial attempts at subtlety failed. She could not take her eyes off Charley, causing Leno to become irritated.

"Come on, Patty. Let's get out of here."

Before she could tell him that she wasn't finished with her burger, Leno was headed out the door. Patty followed behind him but made eye contact with Charley before walking out the door. They had not even spoken a word yet she already knew that she wanted to meet this soldier of rank, especially if he had any chance of becoming the new Camp Director.

CHAPTER 14

Patty had a hard time falling asleep that night. All she could think about was how to meet Sergeant Crambrink. Lying in bed, she quietly laughed to herself as she realized that she didn't even know his first name but she was excited to find out. The next day Patty devised a plan that would allow her to fortuitously meet him. At least, that is what she wanted him to think. Based on what Leno told her the night before, Patty knew that Sergeant Crambrink worked until 6:00 p.m. However, this posed a problem for her because she also worked until 6:00 p.m., which meant that it was impossible for her to be at the Assembly Center by the time that Sergeant Crambrink would be walking out of the building. But she had to make it work because it was the only place she knew he was guaranteed to be at a specific time.

At 4:30 p.m., Patty told her dad that she was sick and asked if she could go home for the day. Her dad believed her to really be sick because Patty never asked off. Her dad knew that she understood that it took every Tagus dollar they could earn to feed their family. Patty ran all the way home. She quickly showered, put her makeup on and slid into the prettiest dress she owned. It was a low cut sage green lace cocktail dress that Patty got secondhand. She looked in the mirror. She was dressed to impress, she thought.

By 5:45 p.m., Patty was waiting just outside the parking lot of the Assembly Center. Several soldiers greeted her as the evening shift arrived for duty and the day shift ended theirs. Leno walked out and saw her, thinking that she was there for him. He attempted to kiss her but Patty turned her face, causing his kiss to land on her cheek. She looked past him, hoping Sergeant Crambrink hadn't seen him kiss her.

Leno asked her what was going on and then realized what she was up to. He remembered how starry eyed she had gotten when Sergeant Crambrink walked into Tad's the night before. Leno thought that Patty's interest in him had been sincere but now he knew that he was obviously mistaken. He shoved her and raised his voice, "It's over between us, Patty. You've just made the biggest mistake of your life."

"Leno, it was over for me before it ever started."

She smiled at him, which further infuriated him.

"I'll personally see to it that no soldier in my command ever goes out with you again. So good luck getting out of this farm town, honey. You'll need it."

Patty rolled her eyes and turned her back to him. Leno marched to the parking lot, got in his car and sped away. Patty had acted as though she did not care. However, Leno's words cut her to the bone. She worried that she had, indeed, made a huge mistake. Up to that point, Patty had not given much thought to the fallout that ending things with Leno could cause. She did not even know this new sergeant and if things did not work out with him, she was worried that she might have blown her chance at leaving Tulare. This was especially true if Leno did not allow any other soldier to date her. There was no doubt in her mind that as a Lieutenant he had the influence to do this. *I have to make it work with Sergeant Crambrink,* she thought to herself. There was no turning back now.

After nearly an hour of waiting, Sergeant Crambrink walked out of the building. Just as the day before, his uniform was perfectly pressed and his eyes barely showed underneath the brim of his dress cap. Patty began walking toward him while purposefully looking back in the opposite direction, toward the parking lot. Her plan to meet him was to quite literally run into him, which would cause him to knock her to the ground and then he would pick her up. Patty slightly leaned forward to brace herself for the impact but because Sergeant Crambrink moved out of her way, she fell flat on her face, skinning up her knee and elbow. Because she was looking in the opposite direction, she did not see

182

Sergeant Crambrink quickly maneuver out of her way to avoid the collision. He turned around and offered to help her up, which she gladly accepted. She was embarrassed, and while her strategy had not worked exactly as planned, it had worked.

"Hello, sir. I don't believe we've met. I'm Patty Attaway."

He tipped his hat toward her with his hand.

"Sergeant Crambrink."

He turned to walk away. Patty did not want this to be a lost opportunity. She made one last desperate attempt to make conversation. "Sergeant Crambrink, aren't you going to at least tell me your first name after saving me?"

Without losing a stride or even slightly turning around, Charley responded:

"I wouldn't exactly say I saved you but if you must know, the name is Sergeant."

As he continued toward the parking lot, Patty didn't know what to do. No one had ever seemed less interested. Patty panicked and ran up to his vehicle just as he arrived at it. She tossed her hair, tilted her head to one side and leaned up against his Jeep.

"Say, do you want to get something to eat?"

She had never been so forward and she immediately regretted it.

"Miss, I don't know you but seeing how you're dressed, you are obviously here to meet someone. The last thing I need in my life is to get between some soldier and his fling. Besides, I saw you at Tad's last night with Lieutenant Jorgensen. I have enough issues with him already. I don't need you complicating that mess."

Sergeant Crambrink got in his Jeep and drove away. Patty was angry with herself. She had messed things up with Leno for this guy, who referred to himself as Sergeant. *Who does that,* she asked herself. To make matters worse, he had the audacity to call her a fling. She was more than offended but rather than allowing her feelings to depress her, they fueled her desire and determination to find a way to show Sergeant Crambrink how wrong he was about her.

Patty went straight home to find her father angry that she was not at home in bed sick as she had led him to believe. When he saw how she was dressed, it only confirmed his suspicions that she had lied. Her dad removed his belt and she knew exactly what that meant.

"Daddy, I'm sorry. Please. I was out with a sergeant who has a real chance of getting me out of here."

"If you were that interested in getting out of Tulare, you wouldn't have ended things with Leno without even telling him. And for your information, a Lieutenant outranks a Sergeant."

Patty's father only priority was putting food on the table. He felt like Patty needed to reorganize her priorities and he had every intention of helping her do that. He grabbed her by the back of the neck, spun her around and gave her a whipping that she would never forget.

"I don't care how old you are. You're gonna learn that your family comes first and that if you're gonna court soldiers, you're gonna do it on your own time."

184

Patty's father refused to let her leave the house for a week except to work in the fields. What Patty couldn't have known about Charley is that he had been in the military long enough to know that any place soldiers were stationed, there were always women willing to do just about anything to have a soldier take them away from whatever their problems were. Charley had also learned that when a soldier took a woman away, it rarely, if ever, meant taking her away from her problems because wherever she went, those problems followed her. Charley had learned early in life that happiness was a choice, despite your circumstances. If someone was unhappy, changing their geographical location or getting married was not going to change that. In many cases, it only made things worse. Charley wanted something more. He wanted to get married someday but to the right person at the right time. He wanted it to matter, to find the one person he couldn't live without, and more importantly, who couldn't live without him. This philosophy always strengthened Charley's resolve when it came to women who wanted to go out with him simply because he wore a uniform.

As the next Friday rolled around, Patty thought the day would never end. The day before was the final day of her grounding. She waited for 6:00 p.m. to arrive so she could go out after work. She had thought all week about how she would approach Sergeant Crambrink again but because she could not leave work early, Patty wasn't entirely sure that she would be able to find him. Patty

185

hoped that just as with the week before, he might be working late. *That's my only chance,* she thought to herself.

After work Patty once again ran all the way home. Just as the week before, she quickly showered, changed clothes and ran out the door. This time, she was more careful and meticulous to fix herself up but not over the top, as she had done the week before. Her makeup was lighter and more subtle and her dress was short sleeved and hung slightly below her knees. It was dark blue with small polka dots, a white lace collar and satin ribbon around her waist. As she looked in the mirror, she felt more like she was going to church than on a date. But she had learned that Sergeant Crambrink was not impressed by fancy clothes.

She walked down to the bus stop, about two blocks from her house, and impatiently waited until the bus finally arrived at the Assembly Center. It was now nearly 7:00 p.m. She was sure that she had missed Sergeant Crambrink. She looked in the parking lot and there were several military Jeeps but Patty couldn't tell one from another. They were all painted drab green with a white star on the top of the hood and some sort of serial number painted on the side of the hood. Patty waited until 7:15 p.m. and realized that she had missed her opportunity. She walked back over to the bus stop. As the bus pulled up, Patty took one last glance toward the Assembly Center and out walked Sergeant Crambrink, putting his hat on as he crossed the threshold of the exit. Her heart started pounding. She turned back toward the bus and closed her eyes, summoning the courage to follow through with what she had been planning all week.

The bus driver addressed her, "Hey, miss. Are you getting on the bus?"

"Not yet."

Patty immediately spun around, trying desperately to not look too eager.

"Sergeant Crambrink, sir, I owe you an apology."

Charley was surprised to see her. For the first couple of days after their initial meeting, he thought she might show up again but when she didn't, he thought she had lost her nerve. Yet there she stood.

"First of all, don't ever call me 'sir.' I'm not an officer. I work for a living. And second, you don't owe me any apology, lady."

Patty didn't like his tone, but at least this time he had referred to her as a lady rather than a fling. She recognized that Sergeant Crambrink was different from most soldiers, which is what attracted her to him. The fact that he had shown absolutely no interest in her made him all the more desirable. However, up until that moment, she had not realized just how different he was. His comment about not being an officer had inspired something in her. He didn't feel that anyone owed him anything. That was so foreign compared to the other soldiers she had dated, especially Leno. Patty understood exactly what Sergeant Crambrink meant. Just like her, it was clear that he had worked for everything he had. This new insight caused Patty to slightly alter her strategy. She decided the only way to win him over was to be real. To be completely honest with him, something that she had never done with anyone, not even herself.

"Sergeant Crambrink, I owe you an apology for my behavior last week but before you say anything, please let me explain. You said that you saw me at Tad's the night before with Leno and you were right. But I also saw you there. In particular, I noticed that you carry yourself different than most soldiers and I just wanted a chance to meet you. The reason I got all gussied up last week was for you, and while childish and immature, I intentionally tried to run into you to meet you, which obviously failed miserably."

Charley laughed.

"I have to admit, I was aware of what you were doing, and while I wished you no harm, I had a good laugh at your expense after I drove away. I have never seen someone fall so hard and get up with so much poise afterward."

This was the first time Patty had seen his demeanor change. He wasn't so rigid and he was right. She had fallen but what he didn't know yet was that she had fallen for him.

"You know, you aren't the first local girl to attempt such a thing to meet a soldier."

"True enough. Sergeant Crambrink, would you please allow me the pleasure of a walk to let me explain? I just want the chance to get to know you a little. Just a walk. That's all it has to be."

"I'm sorry but I have plans this evening."

Patty's head dropped. Her hopes were dashed and she felt like she had, once again, made a fool of herself. However, Charley appreciated her honesty and candidness. He knew from personal experience the courage it took to be vulnerable with someone, especially after the way things had gone the week before, and he admired that. The dress she was wearing also appealed much more to him than the fancy dress she had worn the week before. He felt like it was a more honest representation of who she was. For the first time, Charley saw a bit of genuineness in Patty, something he felt was lacking in most people.

"Patty, there is no need to apologize. If you haven't figured it out already, I don't have time or patience for games. But if all you're really looking for is a walk and a bit of conversation, meet me at Mooney's Grove tomorrow night at 7:00 p.m. sharp."

Mooney's Grove was a beautifully wooded park on Mooney Boulevard between Visalia and Tulare. Patty looked up at him. She was gleaming. By the look on her face, Charley could tell that his offer was completely unexpected. She attempted to muster something intelligent but the only thing that came out was, "See you there."

After continuing toward his Jeep, Sergeant Crambrink cracked a smile, enjoying the effect he had had on this sweet unsuspecting young woman. Just before he entered the parking lot, he halfway turned around. "By the way, you can call me Charley and our meeting is absolutely classified. No exceptions."

189

He looks like a Charley, she thought. Patty took the rest of the evening to walk back home. It gave her time to mull over the events of the evening. Patty knew that things had started off rough but she was finally getting somewhere. She was elated that he had asked her out. The only thing Patty wasn't pleased with was the fact that she could not tell anyone about it. Patty was known for telling all but she did not dare risk messing up the one opportunity she'd barely managed to create.

For Patty, the next day of work was much like the day before. The day seemed to drag on. When it finally did end, Patty went through the same routine as the day before. She hurried home and showered but found it very difficult to figure out what to wear. Her brief experience of Charley told her that he did not appreciate the finer things in life. He liked things simple, which actually made him more complicated, more appealing. He was unlike any soldier she had ever known.

Patty went through her mother's closet and grabbed her mother's Sunday dress. It was dark red with short sleeves, two buttons at the collar and hung just past her knees. It worried Patty that the dress might be overly simple and not impress Charley but she knew she would have no chance with the fancier, more revealing dresses that she owned. Patty went to the bus stop and got on the bus going toward Visalia. There were several couples on the bus out for an evening on the town, including one soldier who Patty had broken things off with to go out with Leno.

He looked at how she was dressed and that she was by herself and sarcastically commented, "No wonder you can't get a date. Look at what you've been reduced to."

Patty bit her lip and refused to turn around. She wanted to tell him that she had a hot date with Master Sergeant Crambrink but the prospect of potentially starting a relationship with Charley was too important to mess up by bragging about the date that he said was top secret.

Patty was the only one to get off the bus in front of Mooney's Grove. It was quiet. She did not see any other people or vehicles. By the time she arrived, it was nearly 7:15 p.m. Patty walked in through the big stone and iron entryway but Tony was nowhere to be found. She was concerned that he either didn't show or, more likely, that he had already left. He was very specific in his directions to be at the park by 7:00 p.m. sharp. That's it! *I've blown my one and only chance,* she thought.

Patty sighed heavily as she turned around to go back out the gates when she heard a familiar voice.

"Giving up so easily?"

Tony had been watching her the entire time from behind a large oak tree. She looked over and he was grinning. Her heart started pounding just as the day before. Patty rarely found herself speechless, yet there she stood. Charley walked over and they began walking through the park. Patty commented on how lush and green the grass was. It was a welcomed change to the dry dusty fields she was accustomed to working in.

Tony did not react to her small talk. Instead, he was direct. "Listen, I'm here because you wanted to go for a walk. What exactly do you want from me?"

Patty grew more uncomfortable with the passing of each second of awkward silence. She wanted to say something, anything, but nothing came to mind.

Charley continued, "It's a simple question. I just want to know what your intentions are."

Patty was flustered. She did not know how to respond. Patty finally answered, trying to make light of the difficult situation. "Well, you are new around here and I thought you could use a friend."

Charley was disenchanted with her answer and she knew it. It was more of a line than a response. He was silent as they continued walking. Patty wanted to ask Charley what he was looking for from her but she worried that he wasn't looking for anything from her. After all, that's how he made her feel in their previous two encounters.

Charley finally broke the silence. "I'm sorry, Patty. This has all been a big mistake but I appreciate you taking the time. I'll give you a ride home."

"Thank you."

Patty didn't know what else to say. She was indeed grateful for his offer to take her home. She knew it gave her one more opportunity to make things right. But as far as Charley was concerned, Patty was like every other woman that had shown any interest in him since joining the Army. Being promoted to Master Sergeant had only increased the attention he received from women.

Patty was angry. She resented the fact that Charley did not seem more interested in her, despite the fact that she was trying so hard. Nothing else was said as they walked all the way to the back of the park where Charley had parked. He assisted her into the passenger side of the Jeep and then got in.

"Charley, you are a difficult person to get to know and I know that I don't always say the right thing, but if you'll just give me a chance, I want to get to know you and I would like you to get to know me."

Patty, demoralized and humiliated, again found herself being completely honest and she didn't like it. It was excruciating for her to open up and share her innermost feelings, especially not knowing if he was going to reciprocate.

"Charley, all I want from you is to get to know you a little and it has nothing to do with you being a Sergeant. I know what most single women in Tulare are looking for from the soldiers, and if you think of me that way, then you are just like all the other soldiers."

Patty rationalized to herself that the lies she was telling were OK because they were things Charley needed to hear to develop an interest in her and it worked. Her words had gotten Charley's attention. She could tell that he did not like being compared to the other soldiers. He prided himself on being different. His view of Patty slowly began to change. *Maybe she really is different from the other women,* he thought. Charley saw two sides to her. He sincerely appreciated her when she was honest and genuine. He thought it made her much more attractive. He decided to give her one more chance. Rather than taking Patty home, he took her up toward the foothills.

When he turned the opposite direction away from her house, Patty wasn't sure what to think but she hoped it was a good thing. Charley did not say anything during the 20 minutes it took to get to where they were going. He found a nice spot near the base of the foothills, almost halfway to Porterville, and turned down a small maintenance road in an orange grove and parked. Patty wasn't sure what his intentions were but she was fully prepared to do whatever it took to secure another date. Charley looked up out of the topless Jeep.

"Sometimes I like to get away from the streetlights of the city to get a better look at the stars."

His speech slowed and his voice became softer and more subtle. "Patty, do the stars ever speak to you?"

Patty lied. "Sometimes."

"What do they say to you?"

Patty thought the conversation was odd, and not wanting to say the wrong thing, turned it back around on him.

"Charley, what do they say to you?"

"Several things."

"I know what you mean."

The fact was that Patty had no idea what he meant. She thought it all a bit strange but well worth the investment to get to know Charley. Just after midnight, he told Patty that he would take her home. While they'd had a rough start, Charley felt like Patty had opened up and been honest with him. She seemed real. They arrived at her house and Charley walked her to the door. She really wanted to kiss him but did not want to press her luck. Then, to her surprise, Charley leaned in and pressed his lips to hers. She was completely caught off guard. She was the first woman he had kissed since arriving in California. He asked if she would like to go out again and she graciously accepted. He told her that he would pick her up Tuesday at 7:00 p.m.

Over the next several days, Patty could not get Charley off her mind. In fact, he became such a distraction that she did everything she could to avoid thinking about him. However, the more she tried, the more she found herself daydreaming. Her thoughts of Charley seemed to make the time go by faster, and somehow slower at the same time, causing the day to drag on. She could not explain it, not even to herself. These were strange feelings she had not experienced before. She talked to her mother about it and her mother told her that she was in love. *How could I be in love,* she asked herself. They had not even really gone out on a real date yet. *Although, he did kiss me.* There was no arguing that. Perhaps her mother was right. Patty told herself that Charlie would be the one that would take her away from all that she hated, away from Tulare and away from fieldwork. And Patty was fully prepared to do whatever was necessary to make that happen.

CHAPTER 15

As Charley arrived at the Assembly Center the next morning he found himself reflecting on the events leading up to meeting Patty. He really hoped that she was as genuine as he believed her to be. He admitted to himself that she was a bit young and immature, but after all she was only 18 -- nearly 19, he rationalized. Still, in those few vulnerable moments when she opened up, there was something about her that appealed to him and he looked forward to their next meeting.

As Charley walked into his office, he was surprised to find Colonel Rose sitting in his chair at his desk. Charley had been suspicious of Colonel Rose since before arriving in Tulare because

Colonel Rose personally requested the orders that required Charley to move to California. Up to that point, Charley's strategy had been to avoid the Colonel at all cost. They had not so much as said a word to each other since Charley's arrival, but now Charley found himself face to face with the Colonel. A conversation was inevitable.

"Shut the door, Sergeant Crambrink, and have a seat."

Charley didn't like his tone but did as he was instructed and shut the door. However, rather than sitting down, he stood at attention, saluting Colonel Rose.

Colonel Rose raised his voice, "I said, sit down, Sergeant."

Reluctantly, Charley did as he was ordered. Charley grew more uncomfortable by the second.

"I've been reviewing your personnel file and your reputation precedes you. However, there are some inconsistencies."

Charley immediately became concerned. *What inconsistencies,* he asked himself. He also wondered why the Colonel had been reviewing his personnel file, especially because Charley knew that his file was unblemished.

"Like what, sir?"

"Well, nothing I have nailed down just yet, but I have been acquainted with other Okies who lied about their age to join the Army due to their, let's call them, humble circumstances."

Having been born at home, Charley was never issued a birth certificate. His social security number was all that was required to enlist in the Army and it was not issued until he was two years old.

198

Besides, his mother and father were dead and to his knowledge, he had no other family that would be able to verify his true age. However, it was obvious to Charley that this Colonel had found something and was out to get him. Charley felt his heartbeat grow more intense. It was the first time he ever considered running away and changing his identity. He knew that if the Army ever found out that he lied about his age to enlist, he would be court marshaled and the Army would prosecute him. He would also be dishonorably discharged. Charley wondered what proof Colonel Rose had found.

The way Colonel Rose used the term Okie, Charley figured that he was like many Californians who saw migrant farm workers, or Okies as they referred to them, as inferior because of their poverty and willingness to do work that no one else wanted to do. Charley actually admired them for this. Like himself, they did whatever was necessary to get the job done and put food on the table. Being an officer, Charley figured that Colonel Rose had come from money and would never understand the reasons why he lied about his age to join the Army. Therefore, he had no intention of admitting his guilt. Charley stood back up at attention, looking past Colonel Rose at the wall, and saluted.

"Sir, I may be an Okie but my birth date as listed in my file is true and accurate. I believe you have me confused with someone else."

Colonel Rose cracked a smile. However, because Tony was looking at the wall, he failed to notice.

"No. I know exactly who you are. That's why I'm inviting you to lunch at my house on Sunday. I've already heard from Lieutenant Jorgensen that you would not be inclined to accept. However, it's an order. I'll see you at 1400 hours. By the way, you have no reason to be concerned, Sergeant."

Colonel Rose got up out of his seat and left his office. Charley realized that he was still saluting and he dropped his hand, confused. *Why would the Colonel order him to have lunch at his house,* Charley wondered. He asked himself what the Colonel was up to. It was all a big mystery and Charley didn't like it. He had no desire to go, but because it was an order he knew that he had no choice. To make matters worse, officers and enlisted personnel rarely, if ever, fraternized and Charley knew that if anyone found out, it would look as if he were kissing up to the Colonel. That was the last thing he needed, yet he knew that no matter how hard he tried, as small as their unit was, word would get out.

Sunday arrived and Charley thought all morning of any excuse he could come up with to not go to the Colonel's house for lunch. However, Charley was not accustomed to making excuses. Few things made him nervous but he did not trust Colonel Rose any further than he could throw him. Charley felt like the Colonel had ulterior motives and he had no idea what they were.

Charley dressed in his Class A uniform and arrived 15 minutes early, just as Charley believed any good soldier would. When Charley arrived at the Colonel's residence, he was impressed but not surprised at its size and how well maintained landscaping was.

After all, he is a Colonel, Charley told himself. The house was two stories with a wraparound porch on the bottom. Charley tucked his hat under his left arm and knocked on the door, believing that he was ready to take on anything that Colonel Rose might throw at him. However, Charley was completely unprepared for what happened next.

A beautiful woman in her early to mid-twenties, with shoulder length brunette hair answered the door wearing a dress that Charley was sure she must have worn to church earlier that day. He still had no idea why the Colonel had summoned him to his home, but all of Charley's concern seemed to fade away in an instant. Charley had never given much thought to love at first sight. However, there was something different that he immediately noticed about the stunning young woman standing before him and it had way more to do than with just her beauty.

"Hello, ma'am. I'm Charley. Colonel Rose asked me to stop by this afternoon."

The woman blushed. She seemed to be just as taken with him as he was with her.

"Please don't call me "ma'am." That's my mother. My name is Annie. Please come in and make yourself at home. My father is expecting you."

Charley thanked her and walked into the living room but continued standing, almost at attention. Annie excused herself to assist her mother in the kitchen. She, along with the rest of the family, was surprised when her father told them that he invited an enlisted soldier to their house because he had never done that before. Charley turned around and noticed Colonel Rose standing at the top of the stairs. He was dressed in casual clothes, wearing jeans and a tucked in button up white shirt. Charley felt guilty for being attracted to the Colonel's daughter and hoped that he had not seen their interaction.

Charley spun around and quickly greeted the Colonel to change the subject of his thoughts. "Hello, Colonel, sir."

"Charley, there is no need for formalities in my home. Call me Jack." Jack smiled and asked, "Do you normally wear your class A uniform to visit people on Sunday?"

"I do if I'm visiting a Colonel's personal residence and I have no idea why."

Charley was uncomfortable. He was uncomfortable calling the Colonel "Jack," he was uncomfortable being at Jack's house and he was uncomfortable having met Jack's lovely daughter.

"Well, Charley, at least take off your coat and stay awhile."

Charley removed his uniform jacket, folded it in half and laid it over the back of the sofa. Jack sat down on one end of the sofa and Charley followed suit, sitting as far from Jack as he could.

"Sir, I don't mean to be rude, but what am I doing here?"

"Well, I told you. I know exactly who you are."

"Who is it that you think I am?"

"Oh, I'm pretty certain you are the son of Pretty Boy Floyd."

You could have knocked Charley over with a feather. He had never shared that information with anyone since joining the Army.

Several questions began to flood his mind. How did he know? What did he want? What did he intend to do with that information? Charley stood up and picked his jacket up off of the couch.

"Sir, I'm not sure who you think I am or who this Pretty Boy Floyd character is, but like I said before, you have me confused with someone else. Good day, sir."

Charley turned to leave when he was interrupted by an outburst of laughter. This only added to his confusion.

"I'm sorry, Charley. I just couldn't pass up the opportunity to get one over on old Charles Floyd, even if it was at your expense."

Jack wiped the tears from his eyes.

"Son, I know you're nervous and confused but it's OK. I knew your daddy. After finally locating you in Chicago, I called my cousin, Dewey, to tell him that I was having you transferred under my command."

"Dewey Padgett?"

"The one and only. Dewey said you were the spitting image of your daddy and he was right. Besides, we all have our debts we owe to Charles Floyd. I intend to pay mine by immediately making you my First Sergeant so I can get that pompous punk, Lieutenant Jorgensen, as far from running the day-to-day operations of my installation as possible."

Charley realized that all of his worrying had been in vain. He was completely shocked that Jack was promoting him to First Sergeant and he was excited about the opportunity. Jack went on to explain that he grew up in Akins and as a child Charles Floyd always gave him a shiny silver dollar.

"You know, Charley, your daddy trusted our family completely, which is why he entrusted Dewey with the coffer chest."

"You know about that?"

"We all knew about it but we respected your daddy way too much to ever attempt opening it. I saw Dewey when I was on leave. I guess it was about a month after you picked it up. I was sorry to have missed you. He told me that you had stopped by right before joining the Army. I've waited ever since for our paths to cross but they never did, so I took matters into my own hands and had you transferred here."

Charley now knew why he was at the Colonel's home and it had nothing to do with the Army. Once again, the father he had never known had intervened in his life. Jack went on to explain that he had attended West Point and received a commission as an Officer because of the benevolence of Charles Floyd.

"In fact, had it not been for your daddy, my family and many others from Sequoyah County would have ended up here in Tulare as migrant farm workers. I owe everything to that man."

Jack's wife walked in and assuming they were discussing Army business, told them, "The time for work is over boys. Come on. Let's eat."

Charley could see where Annie got her good looks.

"Hello, Charley. My husband has been talking about you for months. It's nice to finally put a face with the name."

"Thank you, ma'am. It is a sincere pleasure to meet you."

While eating lunch, Annie adjusted herself to one side of her chair and the wooden chair creaked. However, it sounded like Annie had an intestinal issue. Everyone at the table stifled giggles while Annie, with a mouth full of food, unconvincingly attempted to explain that it was the chair. Under normal circumstances, Annie would never have spoken with her mouth full, especially with such a handsome guest sitting in front of her. However, she felt an overwhelming sense of urgency due to the nature of what everyone thought she had done. It gave everyone a good laugh and broke the ice to get a conversation started.

From that moment, Charley felt as if he and the Rose family were old friends. He learned that Annie was just under a year older than he was and that she was a nurse at Visalia Municipal Hospital. Charley was impressed. He waited all afternoon for an opportunity to talk to Annie alone but it never presented itself. After telling everyone goodbye and thanking Mrs. Rose for the meal, he went to leave. To his surprise, Annie accompanied him out on the porch. She had also been looking for the right moment to talk to him alone. They both began to speak at the same time and laughed as they interrupted each other.

"You go first, Charley."

He loved the sound of her voice. *It's like hearing my favorite song*, he thought.

"Can I call on you in the next day or so?"

"Well, first of all, you'd have to ask my daddy and even if he did allow it, I have a strict rule against going out with soldiers."

Annie smiled, winked at him and then took one last look at him before walking back in the house. Charley knew that he was falling for Annie. She was lovely and he liked the way he felt when he was around her. In the one day he had met and talked to her, she had already inspired him to be a better person.

CHAPTER 16

The next morning Charley was waiting for Jack when he arrived at his office for work. When Jack saw Charley, he smiled and rolled his eyes.

"Oh, boy, I know what this is about."

Charley wasn't sure if Jack was irritated or just giving him a hard time.

"Sir, if it's OK, I'd like to call on Annie."

Jack laughed. "You know, my wife and I had this very discussion last night after you left. We saw the way the two of you were looking at each other."

What Charley didn't know was that Annie had already gone to her father earlier that morning and asked if she could go out with Charley. So it was no surprise to Jack that Charley was there waiting for him when he got to work.

"I'll tell you what. I've always prohibited any soldier under my command from dating my daughter. I know exactly what those guys are looking for and my daughter's not going to have any part in it. However, because of who you are and because I believe that your intentions are sincere, I will allow it under one condition."

"Name it, sir."

"Don't you ever, and I mean ever, break her heart."

"I promise, sir. That will never happen."

At that moment, Jack got a serious look on his face as he pointed at Charley.

"Seriously consider that promise Charley, because I will hold you to it."

"Absolutely, sir. Thank you so much. I won't let you down."

"It's not me I'm worried about."

"I understand, sir."

After work, Charley stopped by the Rose residence to call on Annie. The first time they went out, Charley took her to downtown Visalia. They ate at a local restaurant and then walked past the local shops, looking in the windows at the carefully prepared displays. Charley thoroughly enjoyed the window shopping. It gave him the opportunity to stare more at the reflection of Annie in the window than at the merchandise. What Charley didn't know was that Annie knew exactly what he was doing and she was flattered.

While walking along Main Street they passed a local flower stand. Charley flipped a quarter to the clerk and pulled a single red rose from a tin bucket and handed it to Annie without saying a word. Annie gladly accepted the rose and pressed it to her face, smelling its decadent scent. She reached down and gently took Charley by the hand. They barely knew each other yet they felt as if they were old acquaintances. That evening, they agreed to go out again the following evening.

The next evening Charley and Annie had a wonderful time getting to know each other over dinner. However, after he dropped Annie off and went home, he found Patty sitting on the front steps of his barracks. She had obviously been crying for a long time, as mascara ran down her face. Charley had forgotten all about her and their planned date that evening. Charley ran up to her and helped her up.

"I'm so sorry, Patty. Something came up and I wasn't able to make it."

"Are you sorry for standing me up or for being out with the Colonel's daughter when you were supposed to be out with me?"

Patty was obviously angry and she had a right to be. Charley knew she must have talked to some other soldier. Within two days, rumors had already spread that Charley had been to the Colonel's house and had gone out with the Colonel's daughter in order to be promoted. That rumor was believed to be confirmed when Colonel

Rose ordered Leno to prepare the required paperwork to promote Charley to First Sergeant. Obviously, the rumors were not true, but Charley knew trying to explain it to anyone was pointless. Life had taught him that people believed what they wanted, regardless of the truth. In fact, when he arrived in Tulare, he wanted nothing more than to be promoted to First Sergeant. However, things had changed and it was no longer as high of a priority, but he certainly wasn't going to turn it down.

Patty dried her eyes and smiled.

"I'm sorry, Charley, for overreacting but I understand why you did what you did. If it got you promoted then it was worth it. Now, you can make it up to me over dinner tomorrow night."

Charley knew that Patty couldn't possibly understand what he was feeling for Annie and the fact that she would even insinuate that he would take advantage of someone just to get promoted angered him. *I was obviously mistaken about her*, he told himself.

"I'm sorry, Patty, but I'm no longer interested."

"How is it possible that you profess to be different from all the other soldiers yet you kiss me, making me feel that we had something special, and now you are no longer interested?"

Charley knew the answer to her question but there was no way to explain it in a way that she would understand.

"Patty, even if I tried to explain it, you wouldn't understand. I'm sorry for asking you to Mooney's Grove and you're right, I never should have kissed you."

Patty walked away wailing loud enough for everyone to hear her. She had never met Annie but of course Patty knew who she was. Everyone knew who Annie was because she was the Colonel's daughter. Patty walked away defeated, knowing that there was no way she could compete with the status and money of the Rose family.

Patty walked down a few buildings to the officer's barracks and asked the dorm guard for Lieutenant Jorgenson. A short time later Leno emerged. Seeing her in tears, he asked Patty what had happened and she told him the whole story. Leno took her in his arms and promised her that he would take care of everything. For several days, Leno had been trying to come up with a plan to get even with Charley for taking the day-to-day operations of the Assembly Center from him.

Monday morning, when Leno had overheard Charley ask Colonel Rose if he could go out with Annie, Leno knew exactly what he was up to. Leno had attempted the same thing in order to get promoted to Captain. However, Colonel Rose had denied his request to date his daughter. Leno wondered how Charley had won the Colonel over, although it didn't matter much. *One way or another, I'm going to make sure that Sergeant Crambrink pays for what he has done,* Leno told himself, and Patty's predicament had just given him an idea.

CHAPTER 17

Over the next several months Charley and Annie spent every available moment together. They especially enjoyed long walks and hiking in the mountains among the Giant Sequoia trees in the national park. On one of their hikes in the mountains, near Camp Nelson, Annie and Charley met a local who told them of a naturally carbonated soda spring in the area.

When they arrived at the spring, Charley and Annie observed what appeared to be boiling water flowing out of a hole in the ground about the size of a watermelon. Charley reluctantly touched the water but it was ice cold. He cupped his hands, dipped them in the spring and drank the water from his hands. The carbonation unexpectedly tickled the back of his throat, causing him to cough and consequently spew soda water all over Annie's shirt. They both started laughing uncontrollably. Annie filled her mouth with the water and purposefully blew it all over Charley. He knew what she was planning to do. He saw it in her eyes but he let her do it anyway. Then Charley got the bright idea to stick his head down the hole to see how long he could stay under. He kept his head under water for over a minute and when he came up, the carbonation had caused air bubbles to form all over his face, popping almost in unison before they were quickly gone. Annie wasn't about to let Charley have all the fun. She quickly dropped her head and placed it into the spring. The icy water took her breath away, causing her to immediately remove her head from the spring, while laughing and coughing. They quickly dubbed their new activity soda heading. As far as they were concerned, life couldn't get much better.

In August of 1942, the Army sent word that they were closing the Assembly Center in September and only a handful of soldiers would remain behind to oversee the transition. However, Charley was not among them. Colonel Rose attempted to use his rank to keep Charley in Tulare. However, no Sergeants were staying behind, which meant that there was nothing that he could do.

When the official word had not come back yet regarding Charley's promotion to First Sergeant, Colonel Rose made good on his promise to promote Charley before he was reassigned. He called in a favor to expedite the process and on August 30, 1942, Charley was officially promoted to First Sergeant. Annie presented him with the ceremonial Army-issued Cattaraugus knife issued to all First Sergeants. She had the words, *"To my love, Tony Charles Arthur Crambrink - Promoted to First Sergeant by Colonel Jack Rose - presented by Annie, August 30, 1942,"* etched into the leather sheath.

All of the other sergeants received orders to go overseas to lead troops into combat zones but that was the last place Annie wanted Charley to go. Colonel Rose was aware that the Army was planning to construct and open a new prison camp in Hawaii but had not yet selected the site. He used his influence to get Charley transferred to Oahu to aid in locating a suitable property for the encampment and assist in its construction. Annie was grateful because it was as far from the war as Charley could get. The only problem was that the recent bombing of Pearl Harbor had knocked out all of the telephone infrastructure on the island, meaning their only means of communication would be through airmail, which would take several weeks each way.

It didn't take the community long to organize and plan a party on the soldiers' last evening in Tulare. The celebration was to honor the soldiers for their service. Everyone was looking forward to it, except Charley and Annie. They wanted to spend their last few hours alone. Late that afternoon, they decided that rather than going to the celebration with everyone else, they would drive to Pismo Beach. It was something that they had been planning for months but hadn't been able to make happen yet. Like everyone else, they just thought they had more time.

Charley and Annie both knew that it was late in the day to go that far for a day trip, but it was all they had since Charley was leaving Tulare the following day. They got in Charley's Jeep and drove two hours to Pismo Beach. When they arrived, they left their shoes in the Jeep and walked down to the beach, hand in hand, sitting just short of the incoming surf. It was less than half an hour before the sun set. Annie's hair floated on the sea breeze as the wind blew it to one side. She laid her head on Charley's shoulder, wondering what their future held. She really didn't care as long as they were together. Shortly after the first star appeared, Charley looked at Annie.

"I love you, Annie."

Annie turned toward him and looked deep into his eyes.

"I know."

Charley knew that she really did know. And he knew that she loved him. They sat for a little while longer until Annie stood, silhouetted by the light of the rising moon, and grabbed Charley by the hand. She was smiling and had a glimmer in her eye that Charley had never seen before.

"Come on, baby."

She reached down with her hands open, ready for him to get up. He placed his hands in hers and stood facing her, wondering if she was hungry.

"You want to get a bite to eat?"

"I have a better idea. Come on, I'm driving."

She reached in his front pocket and took the keys from him, giggling. He knew that it was against regulation for her to drive his Army-issued Jeep, but in that moment he didn't care. Just a few miles down the road Annie pulled in to a small local motel. Charley was shocked.

"Aren't we headed back to Tulare tonight?"

Annie looked at him, smiled and then winked. He loved it when she winked at him.

"You can head back tonight if you want, Sarge, but I'm staying right here."

Annie got out of the Jeep, leaving Charley behind and went inside to check into a room. She walked back out twirling the room key around her finger. She found Charley leaned up against the driver's side of the Jeep.

"Annie, if you're planning on spending the night, we don't have any clean clothes, toothbrushes or anything."

Annie was still twirling the key around her finger and she had a grin on her face.

"Well, like I said, you can do what you want, but I'll be in room 222 if you want me."

Charley had never seen her act this way but it excited him. He followed her up the stairs and into the room. Immediately upon closing the door, Annie turned around and began kissing him. Annie ran her hands up his shirt and then lifted it off as Charley put his hands over his head. Annie turned around and held her hair above her neck. Charley kissed her on the back of the neck and

216

without saying a word, unzipped the back of her dress, letting it fall to the floor. She stood there letting him look at her. She was so much more beautiful than he ever imagined. Charley gently pushed her onto the bed and they made sweet, passionate love for the first time. Afterward they held each other until Annie fell asleep. Charley could not believe he had met someone like Annie. He knew that there was no denying that he had fallen deeply in love with her and wanted to spend the rest of his life with her.

Annie woke up a few hours later feeling better than she ever had. She was not sure what time it was but the sun wasn't up yet. She was surprised to find herself alone in bed and wondered where Charley had gone. She slid her dress back on and looked out the window, noticing that the Jeep was gone. She started to get concerned until she saw him drive up. As he came up the stairs, he was carrying a paper bag in each arm and Annie watched him struggle to place both bags in one arm to open the door.

Annie waited for Charley to figure it out and then, just as he got the key in the door, she opened it laughing.

"Do you need some help with that?"

"You've been watching me the whole time, haven't you?"

"What do you think?"

She laughed out loud and planted a big kiss on him.

"You hungry?"

"Famished."

"The only thing I found open was a Mexican place."

"Great. I love Mexican."

Charley pulled several fish tacos out of one of the bags with chips and salsa. The tacos were delicious. They were filled with cod, pico de gallo, cilantro and cabbage. As Annie finished her third taco, she asked Charley what was in the other bag. Charley grinned.

"That's for after we're done eating."

"In that case, I'm done now."

"Then come on, the sun isn't up yet."

Charley grabbed the other bag, took Annie by the hand and headed out the door. They walked down several flights of stairs as they made their way back down to the beach. They walked about a half a mile down the beach, as far as they could go, until the rock face touched the water, cutting the beach off from the other side and forming a small cove. Charley knelt down and began taking the items out of the paper bag. There were two candles, matches, cardboard cut from an old box, scissors, a flashlight and quick drying contact cement.

"What are we supposed to do with all of this?"

Charley looked up at the stars.

"Annie, do the stars ever speak to you?"

She looked up without saying anything at first. She then looked at Charley staring at the stars. Annie gently took his face in her hands, forcing him look into her eyes. *Annie has such beautiful eyes*, Charley thought to himself.

"All the time, my love. And ever since I was a little girl, they seemed to whisper..."

Charley finished her sentence, "That your soul mate not only existed but was looking for you."

"Exactly."

Annie wasn't surprised at all that he was able to finish her sentence. They both had the uncanny ability to know what the other was thinking. He then leaned toward her and she met him the rest of the way and kissed him. They turned their attention back to the items that Charley had pulled out of the paper bag. Charley explained that they were making paper boats. After coating the bottom of his boat with wax from the hot candle to waterproof it, Charley placed the candle in the center of the boat and watched as Annie made hers. *He's obviously done this before,* she thought to herself, as his boat was much more elaborate than hers. Annie affixed her candle to the center of the cardboard boat with some of the candle's wax and they both set their boats out to sea. They watched the boats for over an hour until the sun began rising behind them and they could no longer see the flames of the candles.

"I love you, Annie. I wrote this for you while you slept."

Charley pulled a piece of paper from his pocket and handed it to her. Annie unfolded it to reveal a poem entitled, *"What Happens Next?"* She read the words:

"My whole life all I wanted was to matter, so
I joined the Army in search of something bigger;
I was promoted again and again,
Until they put me in charge of a platoon of men;
At that point, I thought I had it all,

Until I met you and head over heels began to fall;

Annie, I love you still and always will;

What happens next, I can't wait to see,

As long as in the end, it's always you and me."

Tears streamed down Annie's face. She reached behind her neck and unclasped the oval shaped gold locket.

"I've been waiting for the right moment to give this to you."

Charley took the locket in his hand and carefully inspected it. It had one word engraved on the front. "Believe."

Charley opened the locket and inside was Annie's picture on one side and a dried petal from the first rose he had given her on their first date, cut neatly to fit the other side of the locket.

"Charley, this locket belonged to my grandmother. When she gave it to me, she told me that if I had enough faith to believe, my dreams would come true and now you have proved her right. I want you to keep this locket with you always. It will keep you safe and always bring you back to me."

As had quickly become their custom, Charley leaned toward Annie and she met him the rest of the way and kissed him. The rising sun signified Charley's inevitable departure later that day. They walked back up to the motel, checked out and drove back to Tulare. Charley asked Annie to accompany him back to his barracks because he had something he wanted her to have. When they arrived, he removed the coffer chest from his foot locker and emptied its contents into his mother's old cheese box before handing the chest to Annie.

"Annie, this is one of the few things I have from my father. I want you to have it."

"I'll cherish it always."

Annie placed the poem that Charley wrote for her and a couple of photos they had taken together inside. They drove to the airport and embraced for the last time. Charley again leaned in and she met him the rest of the way for that last passionate yet painful kiss. Tears streamed down her cheeks, wetting both of their faces. As he started to pull away, she put her hand on his face and pulled him in tighter before the last call was made for Charley to board the plane. True to her word, Annie wrote Charley every week and sometimes more. Charley cherished every letter and replied to each one he received from her.

CHAPTER 18

As soon as Charley left Leno set his plan in motion to befriend Annie in her difficult and vulnerable time of need in an effort to get even with Charley for taking command of the Assembly Center and Patty from him. The second part of Leno's plan included transitioning his friendship with Annie into something more. However, after the first time Leno attempted to kiss Annie, she shoved him away and told him to get out of her house. The next day he returned with a bouquet of multicolored carnations and asked her to forgive him. He explained that he was just caught up in a moment of weakness and his only desire was to comfort her.

"Annie, you are my best friend and I would never do anything to jeopardize that. Please forgive me."

Annie forgave him, which unbeknownst to her, allowed Leno to continue his vengeful pursuit. Leno learned that winning Annie over was going to take a lot more time and patience than he initially thought. However, with Charley out of the picture, he knew it was only a matter of time. Leno was also aware that if he could get Annie to marry him, it would greatly benefit his career, especially if her father were promoted to General. To accomplish all of this, Leno implemented several strategies.

About a month after Charley left, Leno began by stealing the letters that Annie placed in the mailbox to be sent to Charley before they were picked up by the Postal Service. He also stole all of the letters sent from Charley to Annie after they arrived in the Rose's mailbox each afternoon. It took dedication but Leno was motivated and he never missed a single letter.

In addition, when Patty's family went back to Oklahoma for a couple of weeks due to the death of her grandmother, Leno spread rumors that Charley had flown her out to Hawaii because they were involved in a serious relationship. After her return, Patty perpetuated the rumors, telling everyone that she was headed back to see Charley again as soon as he had more leave. The rumors spread through Tulare like wildfire. By the time they circled back around to Annie, she didn't believe a word of it. While she was a strong person, it became increasingly harder to live in a community where everyone seemed to know everyone else's business. However, none of this deterred Annie from writing Charley. Even when she believed that he stopped sending letters

223

because she wasn't receiving them, she continued to believe that Charley would come back to her and they would be married.

In early February, the weather in Honolulu was gorgeous and Charley was on his way to the airport to pick up a new group of soldiers. They were being transferred under his command from the mainland and as usual, he was anxious to pick up the weekly airmail, hoping to receive a letter from Annie. He had not heard from her since November, which worried him. Initially, he believed her silence to be related to a problem with the airmail. The only problem with that theory was that he continually got letters from Patty, even though he never answered them. She wanted to pursue a relationship with him but he had no interest. Despite not hearing from Annie, Charley continued writing her weekly begging her to reply.

Charley arrived at the airport but the plane had not yet landed. After showing his credentials to the military police officers at the gate, he parked his Jeep on the tarmac. This was against regulations but Charley was in charge of the entire operation and therefore could do what he wanted without question. When the plane landed, the fresh group of soldiers exited. The co-pilot carried the mail bag to Charley and they exchanged the incoming and outgoing mail bags. Charley had two letters in the outgoing mail bag and he hoped there was some form of correspondence from Annie. He pointed to a canvas covered military transport truck and told the soldiers to get in and follow him to their new post.

As they were loading up in the truck, Charley recognized one of the soldiers that had been in his platoon at the Assembly Center in Tulare. Charley motioned for the soldier to ride with him. He headed toward the Army base with the truck full of soldiers following closely behind and began quizzing the soldier sitting next to him.

"What duty station are you coming from, soldier?"

"I was one of the few that stayed behind in Tulare to assist with the transition, but now that it's complete, I, along with just about everyone else, received orders to leave, sir."

"Do you know where Colonel Rose was transferred?"

"You haven't heard?"

"We don't get a lot of correspondence out here. Heard what?"

"The Colonel was promoted to General and chose to stay in Tulare to oversee the operation of Rankin Field."

Rankin Field was the Army Air Corps base in Tulare. The soldier started to snicker:

"Sir, did you happen to hear what Lieutenant Jorgensen did to get promoted to Captain?"

"What? He got promoted? Who promoted him?"

"Well, sir, I heard that you went out with the General's daughter a couple of times but after you left, Lieutenant Jorgensen knocked her up and got promoted to Captain. I heard that they're engaged now."

Charley was livid at the audacity that this soldier had to spread such lies. He abruptly stopped the Jeep on the side of the road, got

225

out and walked back to the truck following behind them. The soldier wondered what Charley was doing, as did everyone else in the truck.

Charley addressed the driver of the truck. "Listen up, soldier. Do you see all those stripes on my arm?"

The driver started shaking. He didn't know where Charley was going with this inquisition but it was obvious that he was angry.

"Yes, sir."

"How many stripes do you count?"

"Six, sir."

"And what's in the middle of those stripes?"

"A diamond, sir."

"What does that diamond mean?"

"That you are the ranking non-commissioned officer on this island, sir."

"Exactly. Now, I'm about to kick that sorry, no good excuse of a soldier out of my Jeep and if you or anyone else in this truck pick him up or attempt to assist him in any way, you'll have to answer directly to me. Is that clear?"

"Sir, yes, sir!"

Charley walked back up to the Jeep and ripped the soldier out of the passenger seat before punching him in the face and kicking him to the curb. The soldier begged Charley to stop.

"If you ever speak that way about the General's daughter again, they will be the last words you ever utter. Now you can walk to base. I don't care how long it takes you or if you ever even find it."

Charley knew that there was no way the information provided by the soldier could even partially be true. And even though he had not heard from Annie in months, he knew there had to be some other explanation. However, over the next several days, a subtle voice inside grew louder that kept asking him how else could he explain why the letters from Annie had stopped. Charley was a man of action. He immediately requested leave due to a personal emergency. As it was more of a formality than an actual request, due to his rank, the leave was immediately approved. Charley went to his barracks, packed and placed the diamond engagement ring that his mother had refused from his father into his pocket. He was going back to Tulare to ask Annie to marry him.

He booked the first commercial flight he could get and landed at the Fresno Airport. Charley could have waited another week until the next military plane was headed back to the mainland but he couldn't wait that long. Upon arrival in Fresno, Charley took the bus to Tulare. The bus stop was several blocks from the Rose residence. He began walking and as he approached the house, Charley saw Annie walk out the front door. He reached into his pocket and pulled the ring out. It was beautiful and he knew that Annie would love it. He had planned to take her to the beach to propose but after all of the mental anguish he had endured, he couldn't wait that long. He was prepared to get down on one knee and propose right then and there.

Charley started walking faster to catch her before she got in the car to leave. But as he got closer, he was heartbroken at what he saw. Annie was definitely pregnant and showing. *The rumors are obviously true,* he told himself. At that very dark moment, Charley hid behind a bush to remain unseen and Annie drove away. He realized that Annie was no different from any of the other women looking to marry a soldier. Because Charley believed that they shared something special, he told Annie who his father was and that his father had left him something that was potentially quite valuable. While she may have been better off than most, Annie obviously had a hidden agenda. He put the ring back in his pocket and vowed never to return to Tulare.

Charley walked back to the bus stop and got on the first bus that came by, not caring where it ended up. Coincidentally, Patty happen to be on that same bus. She could not believe that Charley was right there in front of her. However, it was obvious that something was bothering him. He was a trained observer and always paid attention to the details, yet he hadn't seen her. She walked over and sat down next to him.

"Hey there, Charley. I've sure missed you. Why have you never answered any of my letters?"

Patty wrote him all the time and Charley realized that she had never given up on him, even though he had never answered even one of her letters. As far as he was concerned, Patty had been more real and honest with him than Annie ever was.

"Listen, Charley, I'm sincerely sorry that things didn't work out between you and Annie. I know you cared for her. Can I at least buy you lunch?"

Charley still didn't answer. He was trying to process everything. What he and Annie had seemed so real. However, he realized that their entire relationship had been a lie. He wondered if Patty's being there was somehow meant to be, because he really needed a friend.

By now, Patty had learned how to talk to Charley. They went to Tad's for a hamburger and she sat next to him in the booth. She comforted him and told him exactly what he needed to hear. He was grateful for her companionship during that difficult time. After lunch, Patty enticed him to a motel room where they spent the night together.

The next day, her dream came true as she said goodbye to her life working in the fields and flew back to Honolulu with Charley. He didn't know what to feel. All he knew was that life had dealt him a bad hand and Patty had stood by him through it all. Within three months, Patty and Charley were married. Within another two months, she was pregnant with their first child.

Two years later, Patty received a wedding announcement from Leno that he and Annie were married. Of course, she shared it with Charley. He wondered why they waited so long to get married. He lied and told Patty that he couldn't have cared less but deep down it ate at him. Charley continued his military career and eventually retired just as he had planned, with 26 years of service. Charley never did hear from Annie again, and while he never mentioned her to anyone, thoughts of her tormented him as they were forever lodged in the recesses of his soul.

CHAPTER 19

By the time Charley retired from the Army, it had been several years since he and Patty had kept up any sort of pretenses regarding their relationship. But over the years, they learned to tolerate one another. Long before he retired, they began sleeping in separate bedrooms, which made things easier because it eliminated certain expectations.

One night, while sleeping alone in his room, Charley had a dream about Annie. He was walking down the street and arrived at her house. The house had become dilapidated and rundown and the yard was full of weeds and other debris. Charley knew that this was not how Annie would have lived, yet she had let herself and everything around her go into a state of disarray.

In the dream, Charley realized that the house and yard were reminiscent of every aspect of her life and she was miserable. As he stood in front of her house in disbelief, Annie walked out and was furious with him, letting him know her state of misery was somehow caused by him. She started crying hysterically and began pounding on his chest with her fists yelling, "How could you do this to me, Charley? I loved you. I thought what we had was real."

Before Charley could ask what she was talking about, he woke up in a cold sweat. *The dream seemed so real,* he thought to himself. It caused Charley to reflect on the time in his life when he believed that things happened for a reason. Having the dream had sparked something in him that he had not felt in a long time. He could no longer bear the burden of not knowing why Annie left him for Lieutenant Jorgenson. He decided that he had to know why. Charley told Patty that he was going on his annual trip and he would be back in a week or so.

"Where are you going this time?"

"Wherever the wind takes me."

"Whatever. I'll see you when you get back."

By this time Charley and Patty had become accustomed to taking separate vacations. Patty occasionally took her sister but Charley always travelled alone. Several people thought it strange that they vacationed without each other, but it worked for them.

Charley always visited exotic places. Places that he and Annie had discussed visiting together someday. While on vacation, Charley always fantasized about what life would have been like had he and Annie stayed together. On one such trip, he traveled to the black sand beaches of El Salvador and hitchhiked all the way across Guatemala to the white sand beaches of Belize. On his way to Belize, he stopped in Antigua long enough to see the active volcano, Pacaya. Charley hiked to the top, past the molten lava, and stood near the edge of the crater as smoke poured out of the top. The heat was so intense that he had to use his arm to shield his face from the heat.

Charley reached in his pocket and pulled out the diamond ring that was first meant for his mother and then meant for Annie. *It's been nothing but a curse to me and my family,* he thought. He read the word that he had engraved on the inside of the band: "Believe."

Charley cringed at the meaning of the word and what Annie had told him it meant to her. He no longer believed in people, his dreams, the stars or anything else. He reared back and threw the ring into the caldera. He then pulled Annie's locket from his pocket and opened it. Charley ran his thumb across her face, holding back the tears. He then closed his eyes and held the locket close to his face to smell the rose petal but the fragrance had faded, just as Annie had faded from his life. He attempted to throw the locket but he couldn't let her go. It wasn't that he didn't want to, but no matter how hard he tried, he could not escape her memory.

Charley lashed out at the volcano. "Take it! I don't want it!"

Charley did not understand life. No matter how much she hurt him, he still loved her. He finally conceded that he would always love her and he hated himself for it. Later, he was grateful that he kept the locket. He passed it down to Heather, although he took the picture and rose petal out of it and replaced them with a picture of himself, Heather and Tony.

Charley began the long journey back to California. He was not sure if he would even find Annie but he believed that if it was meant to be, he would find her. If not, he convinced himself that he would find solace knowing he had tried. However, deep down he knew that wasn't true. Charley wanted to see her. He wanted to know what he had done to cause her to leave him for Leno.

Charley planned to start by visiting Annie's mother. He knew that after her father retired from the Army, they moved to Oceanside, near Camp Pendleton. Charley got their address from a previous commander he had served under who also knew General Rose. Unfortunately, when Charley called the former commander, he learned that General Rose had recently passed away. Charley ached for Annie. He wished he could have been there for her.

Rather than flying directly to Oceanside, Charley flew into Fresno to visit his old stomping grounds. He was hoping it would help him put things into perspective. Charley made his way from Fresno down to Visalia and went past the old Tad's Drive-In. It was now called Mearle's Drive-In and was painted bright pink. He stopped and had a burger but it wasn't even close to the same.

Charley made his way to the Tulare County Fairgrounds where all of the barracks and Army offices had been. They were all gone. Even the Rose's residence had been replaced by an outlet mall and movie theater next to a new highway. *So much has changed,* he thought.

He left Tulare and headed south toward Oceanside. Charley arrived and parked more than a block away from Mrs. Rose's residence. He walked down the street and saw a man outside on a ladder painting the house. Charley asked the painter if Mrs. Rose was home. The painter came down the ladder and in broken English explained that she would not be home until later that afternoon, but that her daughter was inside. Charley's stomach dropped and a lump formed in his throat.

"You mean Annie is here right now?"

The painter told him that he didn't know her name but she was a doctor, which confirmed to Charley that Annie was inside. *She actually fulfilled her dream of becoming a doctor.* Charley was so proud of her. The painter asked Charley for his name and he reluctantly provided it.

About ten minutes later, Charley saw someone emerge from the front door. It was Annie. She was so beautiful, yet obviously not as young as he had remembered. Her long brunette hair hung in the wind about midway down her back, held back out of her face by sunglasses sitting on top of her head. She was wearing shorts, a tank top and flip flops. After so many years apart, the only thing standing between them was a wrought iron gate.

"Charley, is it really you?"

Charley couldn't answer. He didn't have the words. He had forgotten the lovely tone of her sultry voice. It made him melt inside. Annie opened the gate and invited him in. They both sat down on the wicker couch on the screened-in porch. Annie told him that before he explained what he was doing there, she had something she wanted to tell him. Charley listened intently.

Annie explained that earlier that same day, for the first time in many years, she took the coffer chest down from the top of the closet and pulled out the few photos she had of the two of them together and read the poem Charley had written her. She then closed her eyes and silently prayed that she could have someone in her life again that she could confide in, who would understand her the way she once believed that he did.

"And now, here you are. I'm not sure how to take that, but I feel the need to tell you what is going on in my life."

Charley still didn't say a word. Annie related that after Charley never came back she was devastated, especially after learning of his marriage to Patty. After more than a year, she finally allowed herself to fall in love again with someone who had helped her in her time of need. Although she admitted that while she knew they would never share the same sentiments that she and Charley once shared, she believed the person to be a true friend. That's when she married Leno.

Annie knew that marrying Leno would help his career because of her father's rank. It was the least she could do for him after he had been there for her in her darkest hours, when Charley was not. After their daughter's sixth birthday and nearly five years of marriage, Leno was promoted to Major. It wasn't long after that

that Annie learned Leno was cheating on her with a newly enlisted recruit working as his secretary.

Annie was lost again and had no one to turn to. She attempted to find comfort at church but was told by her pastor that no one was perfect, people make mistakes and that she needed to forgive her husband so that they could move on with their lives. As difficult as it was, Annie decided to do just that. She knew that a divorce would be devastating to their daughter, especially if she were to learn what Leno had done.

"Forgiving Leno and staying with him after what he did to me was the hardest thing I have ever done, second only to losing you. My father's death was difficult but it pales in comparison."

Charley was so confused. He had so many questions, but he waited for Annie to finish. Annie explained that she had learned earlier in the week that Leno was cheating on her again. That was the reason she and their daughter were visiting her mother until she could figure out what to do. Annie was angry with herself for being naive enough to believe that it would never happen again.

"So, Charley. Now you are here. Tell me why. Why now, after all these years?"

Charley wanted to ask her why she stopped writing him and why she had thrown everything away to be with Leno. Instead, he decided to answer her question. Charley told her about his dream. He then told her that trying to get over her was the hardest thing he had ever attempted but that he had failed miserably.

237

"People say that time heals all wounds but I have never healed. Not from this, because the truth is I still love you."

Charley scooted over next to her and leaned in to kiss her. But this time, with tears streaming down her face, Annie did not lean in to meet him the rest of the way. She wanted so badly to believe him. She wanted to believe that God had sent him there to comfort her and take care of her. How else could she explain his dream that led him to her on the very day that she prayed to have someone to talk to? But all she felt was lost and unsure of herself.

"Are you still married to Patty?"

Charley leaned back away from her and looked down but didn't answer. Inside, Annie knew the answer. However, it really didn't matter because regardless, she was married to Leno and that was a commitment she took very seriously. She wasn't about to cheat on him even if she was sure that their future together was over.

Annie stood up and raised her voice. "Why didn't you come back? I waited for you for almost two years."

Charley's questions came back to his mind. "Why did you stop writing me? I wrote you every week for months with no reply. And I did come back after I heard about you and Leno all the way out in Hawaii. How you guys got engaged because you were pregnant with his baby and within just a few months of my transfer to Hawaii. But I knew there was no way that could be true. So I came back here to ask you to marry me and then I saw you and you really were pregnant. How could you do that to me, especially after knowing how I felt about you? For me, it was all real."

"It was real for me too, Charley."

Annie sat back down and took a deep breath.

"Charley, that baby I was pregnant with, well, she is your daughter."

"What? What are you... What do you mean? How can that be?"

"Don't you remember that night at the beach? Lora is your daughter."

Charley lowered his head, trying to comprehend what he just heard. He knew that Annie would never lie to him. The dream he'd had was true. *It was me that ruined both of our lives. It wasn't Annie.* All of the hurt and anger that he had carried for the past 15 years was from his own assumptions and because he refused to confront Annie all those years ago. He had not given her the benefit of the doubt or at least enough credit to ask her in person. And he had a daughter that he had never even known about.

"Annie, why did you never tell me we had a daughter?"

"I wanted to tell you in person. I thought I knew what we had. I kept telling my parents not to worry about us not being married yet because there wasn't any doubt in my mind that you would be back the first chance you got. I knew we would be together no matter what and that she would be a great surprise for you. I even named her Lora, after your mother. Then, shortly after she was born, I found out you and Patty were married. You think you've had it hard? Charley, you have no idea."

239

The phone inside rang. Annie left the porch and went inside, grateful for the interruption. She came back out with the phone up to her ear. It was Leno. He wanted to know when she was coming home.

"Let me ask you a question, Leno. Did you have something to do with my letters to Charley disappearing?"

There was a pause while she listened to Leno.

"How could you? I don't even know who you are. Well, guess what? I'm here with Charley and he just told me that he loves me."

Annie hung up the phone and started crying.

"He burned them. He burned them all."

Instantly Charley knew exactly what had happened and why. Leno had promised Charley that he would pay, and now he knew that Leno had won. It was also obvious that Leno had taken their letters all those years ago and burned them in order to take Annie from him, and Charley allowed it to happen. *I never cared much for Leno anyway, but now I hate him,* he thought. Charley had caused his own heartache for all those years, but to make matters worse he had devastated his dear sweet Annie.

Annie sat back down and wiped the tears from her face. "Charley, I've needed you so much over the years, but you weren't there for me like you promised. I did what I had to in order to survive."

Just then the most precious red-headed young woman that Charley had ever seen walked out onto the porch.

"Mom, is everything OK? I heard you yelling."

"Everything is fine, baby. I was just visiting with an old friend when your father called and upset me. I'm sorry for disturbing you. Go on inside sweetie and I'll be in shortly."

Lora stood in the doorway, staring at Charley.

"Lora, sweetie, go on back inside and I'll be along shortly."

Finally, Lora did as her mother requested and went back in the house.

"Annie, she's beautiful."

"Charley, she knows nothing about you and as much as it pains me to say this, that's the way it has to be. You chose this for all of us and now we must all bear the consequences. I don't ever want her to feel the abandonment and loneliness that I felt when you never came back. Finding out that Leno is not her father would devastate her. She deserves better than that and you at least owe me that."

Charley knew she was right and there was nothing he could do to change that. He leaned over and touched his forehead to hers.

"I am so sorry, Annie. For everything. I know nothing I could ever do would make any of this right."

"Charley, did you really believe back then that we were meant to be together?"

"You know I did."

"I know. I just needed to hear it one last time before you left."

Charley could not ask for Annie's forgiveness. He didn't deserve it and he knew it, nor would he ever be able to forgive himself.

Charley returned home to Patty and his two boys, Hank and Dave. *What else could he do,* he thought to himself. There was no other answer and no way to go back in time to change things. Up to that point he had always believed himself to be an honorable man, but now he had to live with the consequences of his decisions. Besides, even if he was willing to leave Patty for Annie, he knew that Annie would never allow it. She would not be the reason for breaking up a marriage, even one as superficial as theirs. There was no other decision for either of them. He carried Annie and Lora in his heart for the rest of his life but never mentioned them to anyone.

CHAPTER 20

When Annie finished telling Heather her story, they both had tears in their eyes.

"You know, Heather, your grandpa taught me that things happen for a reason and I still believe that. I don't pretend to know all the reasons why things happened the way they did but I have faith that someday I will have a greater understanding, even if it's after this life."

Heather pulled Grandpa Charley's letter out of her pocket and shared it with Annie. It was the same letter that led Heather to Annie's house.

"Annie, I still don't understand what Grandpa Charley meant when he told me not to make the same mistake that he did."

"Heather, dear, I don't mean any disrespect to Patty, but Charley is telling you that if you don't go after the person who is the most important person in the world to you and make a life with him that you will regret it forever. Something Charley and I know all too well."

"He means Tony, doesn't he?"

"Heather, only you can know that."

"I was afraid you'd say that. He definitely means Tony."

Things had never been clearer to Heather and she knew what she needed to do. Annie smiled, knowing that Heather had found the clarity that she was looking for.

"It really is amazing to me that Grandpa Charley set all of this up years ago."

"Well, there are a few more things I need to share with you. Do you know if Tony found the small rose colored stone that Charley left in the ammo can?"

"Yes. I saw him take it out of the ammo box. What is it?"

"Charley broke it off his father's tombstone and hid a strong magnet inside. Charley designed it be placed against the pole sign that he built at the corner of his property."

"You mean Iron Post Corner?"

"Yes. I believe that is the name of it. There is a false compartment at the bottom that is only accessible when the magnet hidden inside the stone is placed against the metal pole. There, you will find what Charley left for the two of you."

"What is it?"

"Honestly, I have no idea. He never told me, but I wish you the best of luck on your journey. I hope you find what it is you're looking for."

Heather hugged Annie and thanked her for all that she had shared. She was excited to be on to the next part of her journey and she couldn't wait to tell Tony what she had learned. Heather knew that he was still in training at the Halliburton Corporate Campus for a few more days before he was scheduled to go back to Venezuela.

In order to change her plane ticket from Baton Rouge to Houston, Heather had to pay nearly the cost of a new ticket but she didn't care. *It was worth it*, she thought to herself. Heather was excited to tell Tony about the secrets contained in Iron Post Corner and to discover the treasures that were contained inside.

She arrived in Houston and drove directly to Halliburton's headquarters. She walked into the lobby and the receptionist greeted her.

"May I help you, miss?"

"Yes, ma'am. I need to contact Tony Crambrink. It's a bit of an emergency and I believe he's here training."

"Hold on just a minute and I'll see if I can locate him."

"Thank you."

A short time later Tony stepped off the elevator with a confused look on his face. He walked up to Heather and quietly asked, "What are you doing here? They told me that there was some sort of emergency."

"Tony, do you have time to walk out to the car with me? I need to show you something."

"Sure. We were about to finish for the day anyway."

Tony followed her to the parking lot, wondering what she was doing there. It was so good to see her, especially because up to that point he didn't know if he'd ever see her again. Heather reached inside her car and pulled out Grandpa Charley's Army-issued dog tags. Tony's eyes widened with excitement as he read his grandpa's name, confirming they really belonged to Grandpa Charley.

"Where did you get these?"

Heather related everything that she learned from Annie, including how to open the vault contained within Iron Post Corner. Tony looked back at the Halliburton building, hesitant to miss the following day's training.

"Come on, Tony. What is there to think about? Let's go. It's what Grandpa Charley wanted."

After all she had learned from Annie, she never thought twice about what the next step was, which is what led her back to Tony. It never crossed her mind that Tony wouldn't feel the same, especially after learning about Annie and all that she had shared. It irritated Heather that Tony even had to think about it.

"Tony, please."

Grandpa Charley's words came to Heather's mind:

"Heather, don't make the same mistake I did or you will regret it forever."

Heather closed her eyes and took a deep breath. *Go all in,* she told herself. She hugged Tony and whispered in his ear, "Please, Tony. Come with me. I can't do this alone. I need you."

Tony pulled away.

"I'm sorry, Heather, but I've moved on. I've got training for the next couple of days and then I'm headed back to Venezuela. To tell you the truth, I don't have any desire to ever go back to the farm again. Besides, I doubt there is anything in that old sign."

The truth was that between having to ask Rich for more time off and not wanting to continue this wild goose chase, Tony just wanted to get back to some sort of normalcy. However, Heather didn't see it that way. Tony's words confirmed to her that Tony was not who Grandpa Charley thought him to be and that he was definitely not for her.

She shoved him and raised her voice. "You are just like your father. Hank would do exactly the opposite of what Grandpa Charley was asking and you know it."

"But I thought…"

"Well, you thought wrong. Just go back to your life and always wonder, what if."

What does she want from me, Tony asked himself. He took the dog tags and turned around to walk away.

247

"I would not have expected any less from you, Tony. You don't deserve Grandpa Charley's name. How dare you walk out on him? I hope I never see you again."

By the time Heather got all of that out, tears streamed down her face. She was so angry but she meant every word. She told herself that she had been right about him all along and she was glad that Grandpa Charley had passed away before realizing who Tony really was. Over the past several days, Heather had come so far and had grown so excited to finish her journey together with Tony. It was hard for her to believe that it was all over, but unfortunately the choice to continue was no longer hers to make since Tony had the stone.

Heather's words had cut Tony to the core. He told himself that she didn't know what she was talking about. *Obviously, she doesn't know me, especially if she thinks I'm anything like my father,* he thought. Tony went back to his hotel and sat on the edge of the bed, the guilt building inside him. There was a knock at the door. It was Oak.

"Hey, Tony, why didn't you tell me your Grandpa Charley passed away? This whole time I've been trying to figure out what was wrong with you. I thought I had done something."

Tony didn't really want to talk about it and attempted to change the subject.

"Aren't you supposed to be in North Dakota?"

"Yes, but I took off a couple of days so I could see you before I headed back. Now, what's the deal? How come you didn't tell me about your grandpa?"

Tony realized that Oak wasn't going to let this go.

"How did you find out?"

"Rich told me the day that he made you take a week off. I went by your room but I guess you were already gone. Where have you been?"

"Of course Rich told you. I wouldn't expect anything less from him. Anyway, I went back to Oklahoma for a couple of days to tie up some loose ends."

"Were you able to take care of things?"

"Yeah, I mean, I guess so."

"What does that mean?"

Tony sighed and gave in. He knew Oak wasn't going to let it go and he felt like it was time to open up to someone. *Who better than his best friend,* he asked himself.

"Come on, Oak. Let's go get something to eat and I'll tell you all about it."

Oak was grateful that Tony was back to his old self. He took Tony to the Venezuelan restaurant on Shepherd Drive. Oak had not had Venezuelan food in ages and he was craving an "arepa" stuffed with black beans with "patacones" or fried plantains on the side.

"Tony, I'm really sorry about your Grandpa Charley's passing. I know you don't talk about family much, but I know he was important to you."

They sat there for nearly two hours talking. Tony had to stop himself several times in order to hold back the tears. He related all that had happened over the past week leading up to the argument with Heather earlier that day. After the trip to Oklahoma, Tony felt that he was doing well suppressing his anger and guilt, but the argument with Heather had caused it to surface again.

Oak sat there quietly listening until Tony finished his story.

"Tony."

"What?"

"What about the treasure?"

That was not the response he was expecting from Oak. When Tony initially started sharing all that had happened over the past week, Tony was concerned that Oak might think he was crazy. However, Tony realized that it was clearly Oak who was delusional.

"Oak, you're missing the point. There is no treasure. It's a fool's errand, just like that treasure you've been wasting your time looking for in Wyoming."

Since moving to North Dakota, Oak had begun searching for the treasure of Forest Fenn. He believed that he had decoded Fenn's poem and he was certain the Fenn fortune was somewhere in Yellowstone National Park. So when Tony mentioned the tie his Grandpa Charley had to Pretty Boy Floyd and the possibility that his Grandpa Charley may have left him something, Oak was instantly ready to drop everything in search of it.

"Tony, you know what you have to do."

"What are you talking about, Oak? There's nothing left to do. I'm headed back to Maracaibo and you're headed back to Williston."

"Come on, Tony. I'll go with you. We can find it together. Just email Rich and tell him you need a little more time and I'll call in sick. We just need a few days. It will be like old times."

"You know Rich is going to say no."

"Just email him when we get back to the room and then let's get on the road."

Oak was super excited. He just knew they were going to find something. Tony was much more skeptical. He was less than convinced that there would be anything in the old iron sign, and if there was he wasn't sure that even wanted it. If anything, he figured that Grandpa Charley had left him the deed to his property, which he did not want. He had no desire to fight with his dad over a piece of property that he no longer valued since Grandpa Charley was gone. There were just too many painful memories there.

Even though Tony believed it to be a waste of time, he felt like the road trip was the least he could do to try and make things right with Oak after the way he had treated him the week before. Besides, Tony knew that Oak was right, it would be an adventure and they would have fun together just as they always did.

When they got back to the hotel, Tony emailed Rich, requesting additional time off, and packed his things. He sat down on the couch and turned on the TV. Oak was irritated that he was not more motivated.

"What are you doing? Let's go."

"I'm waiting to see if Rich is going to approve my leave request."

Oak reached over, closed the laptop and turned the TV off.

"Come on, Tony. It's better to ask forgiveness than permission."

Tony wasn't sure that he agreed, but he grabbed his suitcase and they headed out the door. They drove for eight hours straight, stopping only for gas. When they arrived in Sallisaw they went straight to Iron Post Corner. Tony placed the stone against the iron pipe and was not surprised when nothing happened.

"See, Oak. I told you. We came all this way for nothing."

"Let me see that."

Oak reached down and grabbed the stone out of Tony's hand. He began moving it up and down on all sides until he heard something moving, as if it were scraping the inside of the pipe. Now he had Tony's attention. Oak continued in the same direction until he heard a click and an entire section of the pipe came loose. He removed the section and found a two-inch cardboard tube wrapped in plastic and capped on both ends that was fairly light. Oak removed it and handed it to Tony. Oak felt around inside the pipe and was disappointed that there was no gold, cash or other valuables inside that would have been tied to Pretty Boy Floyd.

"I told you there wasn't any treasure, Oak."

Tony opened the folder and pulled out a letter to Annie, the mysterious woman that Heather had told him about. There were also several legal documents naming Tony and Heather as executers of Grandpa Charley's trust, which included the deed to Grandpa Charley's property. However, it was not Grandpa Charley's farm as Tony expected it to be. According to the legal description, it was a piece of property located in East Baton Rouge Parish, Louisiana, which listed him and Heather as the owners. Tony smiled, realizing that Oak had been right about one thing. Tony now knew exactly what he needed to do. He also knew who he wanted to be with, if she would have him.

CHAPTER 21

Tony felt guilty for unlocking the vault without Heather. He still wasn't sure what Grandpa Charley was up to or why he gave them property in Louisiana. However, Heather was already there and Grandpa Charley had always said that there was no such thing as coincidence. Tony looked forward to the opportunity to make things right with Heather since their last words had been in anger. He also needed to deliver the letter to Annie and he had no idea where she lived or how to find her. But he knew that Heather did.

Oak drove all night and got them back to Houston early the next morning. Tony was surprisingly rested, having slept most of the night in the car. He dropped Oak off at the airport and then headed for Louisiana. The drive gave him time to think about what he would say to Heather. He finally admitted to himself that he had always loved her.

Tony arrived in Baton Rouge that evening and checked into a local hotel. He desperately wanted to find Heather but he knew that he had no way to find her because he had no idea where she lived. Tony wanted to apologize and tell her how he really felt about her. However, after their last encounter, he wasn't sure how she was going to react. Tony also hoped that Heather could help him locate the property that Grandpa Charley had left them because there was no address, just a legal description.

The next morning Tony found Heather in her office. He stood in her doorway while her back was to him. He didn't say anything but somehow she instinctively felt his presence and turned around. She could not believe he was there. Tony walked up to within about two feet of her and just stared. In that moment nothing else mattered as he placed his hand on her face.

"You are so beautiful. There is so much I need to tell you if you'll just give me the chance."

Heather smiled.

"Yeah, yeah. We'll get to that."

Heather closed her eyes and leaned toward him. He met her the rest of the way and they kissed. Her lips were softer than he remembered. *She smells good,* he thought to himself as he finished the kiss and looked back at her.

"So what do you have to tell me?"

"First of all, that I'm sorry. Sorry for everything. I hope you can forgive me."

"I already did."

"The other thing I have to tell you is that I have no idea what or where this is."

Tony pulled the deed from the folder and handed it to Heather. Heather took the paper and began to read. Her eyes widened as she read the front page of the deed. She could not believe what she was holding. She turned the page and continued reading the legal description. She turned back to the first page to verify that it belonged to her and Tony. *Could it really be,* she asked herself. Heather sat down at her desk, grabbed her necklace and stared at the wall. It was obvious to Tony that she was in deep thought.

All of a sudden, Heather mumbled something that Tony could not make out.

"What was that?"

"I said, it can't be."

"Can't be what?"

"Come with me."

Heather jumped up and headed out the door. She was moving so quickly that it was all Tony could do to keep up with her. Tony had no idea where they were going but he was happy to accompany her wherever she wanted to go. As they drove away from LSU, Heather seemed to know exactly where she was going. He smiled as he realized that Heather always seemed to be at least one step ahead of him. He was OK with that.

Heather turned onto Highland Road and Tony noticed that the further they went the tenser Heather seemed to get. What Tony didn't know is that Heather felt like she was going to throw up.

"Heather, are you OK?"

She did not speak. She just nodded in the affirmative and continued onward. But the truth was that Heather was not all right. There were very few times in her life when she couldn't speak but this was one of them. *Had Grandpa Charley really done this,* she wondered. She questioned how it was possible. However, if he did somehow pull it off, she knew that Grandpa Charley had been right. Without even knowing it, this is exactly what she wanted.

As they arrived at the far corner of the property, Heather was pleasantly surprised to see how lovely and well-kept it was. Someone had obviously taken great pride in keeping it well-manicured and groomed. It looked better than she remembered. Heather approached the driveway and noticed a sign that had not been there before. It was relatively new looking with a wagon wheel in the center of it. Above the wagon wheel were the words:

"McDuff Plantation Bed and Breakfast."

When Tony saw the name of the bed and breakfast, he began putting the pieces together. Heather turned down the driveway and parked the car. The house looked just as she remembered but a bit newer, as if it had undergone a mild restoration. The red brick covering the house looked brighter, the matching tile roof that used to be covered in mold looked new and there were several more plants growing in the courtyard, along with four big potted ferns hanging from the large front porch. The brick wall surrounding the courtyard was still covered in woodbine honeysuckle, which was in full bloom. Heather closed her eyes and inhaled, taking in the sweet scent. *I'm home,* she thought to herself.

As they walked in through the gate, Heather could not help but see her daddy sitting on the porch in a rocking chair waiting for her to arrive off the school bus. She had so many memories here. She had not realized how much she had missed this place. The tire swing that once hung from the largest branch of an old oak tree had been replaced by a large porch swing. Heather grabbed the chain of the porch swing to steady herself, turned around and sat down. Tony sat beside her. Heather looked at him as a tear rolled down her cheek.

"I haven't been here since I was a kid."

"Why haven't you ever come back? Isn't your daddy buried around here somewhere?"

"Tony, there is something I need to tell you and it may greatly change your opinion of me. Please don't say anything. Just let me get it out."

Heather closed her eyes, pushed the swing backward with her legs and something unexpected happened. The memories began to settle on her mind like soft summer dew.

When Heather was nine years old, she arrived home from school one afternoon. The bus dropped her off at the end of the driveway and she ran all the way up to the front porch, where her daddy greeted her. He promised her that if she got an "A" on her spelling test, he would take her to Lafitte to go gator hunting. Heather's daddy loved the thrill of the hunt. To hear her daddy tell it, gator hunting was exhilarating.

Heather had waited for as long as she could remember to be old enough to hunt gators with her daddy. She had only been once. It was the last day of the season the year before but they did not catch any gators that day. Heather was disappointed when her daddy said, "Well, there's always next year."

But to a little girl, a year felt like forever. Finally, the time had come and rather than it being the last day of the season, it was the first. Her daddy had already baited the hooks earlier in the day and drove back home to get her. He knew how smart his little girl was, not to mention she had been studying for a week straight. Heather ran up onto the front porch.

"Well, baby, how did you do on your test?"

"I got 100 percent."

Heather's daddy scooped her up in his arms and threw her up in the air. He was so proud of her.

"Now hurry up and get changed so we can get on the water before dark."

They drove two hours south, where their small aluminum boat was tied to the dock at Lafitte Harbor, right where her daddy left it. It was the only boat left at the dock. Everyone else was already out checking their lines. Heather's daddy strapped her life jacket on and they started down the canal and into the bayou. The first two hooks they checked hadn't been touched. However, the third line was in the water and tight.

"Now be careful, babe. This one has a live gator on it. I'm going to grab the line first and then you help me pull her in after I set the hook."

"OK, daddy. I'm ready."

Heather remembered feeling the rush of adrenaline take over as her daddy yanked the line to set the hook. She reached up and grabbed the thin black nylon cord to help her daddy pull the gator in but when the hook set, the gator rolled and the line slipped out of her daddy's hands.

"Baby, let go."

But Heather did not let go. She was immediately thrown overboard into the water. Her daddy dove in to save her as the gator thrashed back and forth on top of the water, attempting to free itself. Heather remembered feeling the severe pain run up her arm when her daddy grabbed her and threw her back into the boat. Heather jumped up just in time to see her daddy go under the brackish water. Even after he was submerged, she could see his silhouette under the water for several seconds. However, there was nothing she could do.

She began screaming, "Daddy! Please come back up! Someone help!"

The cord wrapped around his arm when he dove in and after he threw Heather back into the boat, the gator swam to the bottom, where it felt safe. This pinned her daddy down underneath the

260

water. A couple of gator hunters about half a mile away could not make out what was being said but they heard the screaming and immediately responded. As they approached the boat and observed a little girl alone crying hysterically, they knew what had happened. One of them jumped in the water, found the cord and followed it to her daddy. The man cut the cord with his knife and brought her daddy's lifeless body to the surface, while the other hunter pulled him into the boat and began CPR. They drove back to the marina but it was too late. Her daddy had been under water too long and did not survive.

After arriving back at shore, Heather overheard the hunters talking.

"He had no business out there gator hunting by himself."

"Yeah, and she is entirely too young to be out there with him. What was he thinking?"

"I don't know, but he's lucky that gator finished him off. Otherwise, he'd be lookin' at child endangerment charges."

Heather opened her eyes, scared of what Tony would think of her. Tears streamed down her face. She turned and looked at Tony and he was just as emotional as she was.

"Tony, I wanted to tell them that it wasn't Daddy's fault. I begged him to let me go gator hunting and when he told me to let go of the line, I didn't do it. It all happened so fast. I killed my daddy."

Heather covered her face with her hands and buried her head in Tony's chest. He put his arms around her and gave her time to get it all out. As Tony gathered his thoughts, he knew the death of her daddy was not her fault. *But how can I convince her of that,* he wondered. He ached for her, knowing that she had carried that guilt for most of her life.

Tony stood up. He gently took Heather by the hand and walked over to the red brick wall of the courtyard where the honeysuckle was the thickest. He pulled a solid apricot-colored blossom from the vine and raised it to his nose and then handed it to her.

"Heather, I sincerely wish your daddy hadn't died that day. There is no doubt that he loved you with all his heart. But he would not want you to carry that burden. I know you feel responsible but it wasn't your fault. There is nothing you could have done. Sometimes things happen that are out of our control."

"Then why do you feel guilty about not being there for Grandpa Charley and not being there when he passed away?"

Heather's question had pierced Tony to his core. She was right. He did feel guilty.

"That isn't fair. I made the decision to take a job out of the country rather than returning to the farm. Besides, I thought you were angry at me for that very thing."

"No. You made the decision to run away rather than face your past, and Grandpa Charley gave you the easy way out by encouraging you to do so. He didn't want you to suffer any more than you already had. He loved you so much. As for me being angry with you..."

Heather paused and looked down at the ground, ashamed for her behavior and thoughts toward Tony over the past several years. She wiped the tears from her face with her hand and continued. "As for me being angry with you, I'm not. Sometimes I think we see in others those things that we dislike most about ourselves, and now I know that I have been taking the anger and guilt I felt for my daddy's death out on you. I'm sorry, Tony."

"Heather..."

Tony was interrupted by the manager of the bed and breakfast. They had not noticed but an employee had alerted him to their presence. Being the kind of establishment that prided themselves on knowing their guests, the employee did not recognize either of them and the manager went to investigate.

"Can I help you?"

Heather immediately answered:

"Um, yes, sir. Who owns the bed and breakfast?"

"Are you guests of the McDuff Plantation?"

"Not exactly but we are interested in staying here. Now, who owns this place?"

The manager thought that her question came across almost like an interrogation. He was a bit apprehensive and careful with his answers.

"The home and property are owned by a trust."

"What is the name of the trust?"

"That information is privileged, ma'am. The owner, who is now deceased, asked that the personal information, including the names of the executors of the trust, be kept secret. I'm sorry but I cannot divulge that information."

Heather presented the manager with the deed that Grandpa Charley had left them and asked if the persons listed on the deed were the sole proprietors of the property. The manager looked over the document and then handed it back to her.

"Please come in and have a seat in the sitting room. I will get someone who can answer your questions."

Nearly 45 minutes later, a middle-aged gentleman arrived and met them in the sitting room. He explained that he was the attorney that represented the trust and asked to see Heather's identification. She realized that in all of the chaos, she left her purse in her office at LSU. Heather started to get irritated until she saw Tony already handing the manager his driver's license. By now, Tony had figured it all out. Grandpa Charley had purchased Heather's family plantation and turned it into a beautiful bed and breakfast in order for it to sustain itself until they could follow the breadcrumbs.

"Thank you, Mr. Crambrink. I assume you are Ms. McDuff, the only living descendent of the original owners of the property."

"I am."

"Congratulations, Ms. McDuff. I have been waiting on both of you for some time. In answer to your question, yes, the property belongs to the two of you. Mr. Crambrink purchased the property and took your advice to turn it into a bed and breakfast."

Heather had forgotten but she once told Grandpa Charley that when they were packing their things to move to Oklahoma, she had asked her momma why they had to leave. When her momma told her that they could no longer afford to keep the property, Heather asked her why they couldn't turn it into a bed and breakfast like so many other plantation homes up and down the Mississippi River. Her mother told her that the residence was too small to support a bed and breakfast.

The attorney continued, "It can continue as a bed and breakfast or you may do with it as you wish. The name of the trust is the Tony Charles Arthur Crambrink trust and it was set up with the intention of running and maintaining this property. Of course, you and Mr. Crambrink are the sole executors of the estate. There are some legal matters to tend to and some documents that need to be signed, but all of that can be sorted out later. Well, now, I'll leave the two of you here. I'm sure you have much to talk about. If you need anything at all, here is my card. You may reach me day or night. Also, as the owners, you are welcome to stay in any of the guest room suites free of charge."

Heather was absolutely speechless and overwhelmed with joy. She had her daddy's place back, something she never dreamed would happen. And, if Tony wanted to... if he wanted her, she would have someone to share it with.

As Tony attempted to muster the courage necessary to kiss Heather again, she leaned in and pressed her lips to his. Tony closed his eyes and experienced a feeling unlike any he had ever felt. The kiss was simple yet passionate.

Heather knew that Tony was the man she had been looking for all of her life. Deep down, she had always known. She acknowledged to herself that she had just been too stubborn to admit it. As they looked into each other's eyes, they knew their futures were intertwined.

Tony silently thanked his Grandpa Charley and then felt his words: "Tony, do you know why thou art confederate?"

Tony whispered back: "Because we are allies, united and banded together, sent here with the purpose of looking out for each other. And Grandpa Charley, thank you for pushing me to follow the breadcrumbs."

When Heather overheard Tony's words, she was shocked.

"What did you just say?"

"It's what Grandpa Charley used to call us as kids, his "little confederates.""

"No, no. After that."

"In my dream, Grandpa Charley told me to follow the breadcrumbs and I felt like that is what led us here."

"Tony, that night in the hospital Grandpa Charley told me to follow the breadcrumbs and they would lead me back to the beginning and I would find the thing that I most desired. Now I'm here with you and we have my family plantation back."

They both realized that everything was true. Things indeed had happened for a reason. Tony also realized that in his dream when Grandpa Charley took him outside to show him what he had for him, Grandpa Charley was not pointing back into the house toward the knife or even toward Iron Post Corner. Grandpa Charley was pointing toward the cemetery where Heather had found him. Heather was the great treasure that Grandpa Charley had for him and Tony now knew that they would spend the rest of their lives on that sacred property where they would continue their beloved Grandpa Charley's legacy.

Heather eventually came to understand that it was Grandpa Charley's intention that night in the hospital to have her save Tony. However, just the opposite was true. Tony had saved her and his beloved Grandpa Charley had given her the man that "...*was a young man of that fineness of blood and lowness of station common to the conventional heroes of romance who love royal maidens.*"

In time, Tony and Heather were married. Eventually, they had twins, a little red-headed boy named Tony III, and a beautiful red-headed girl named Anne Elise, who they called Annie. Heather and Grandpa Charley were finally family. She was a real Crambrink. However, in her heart, she knew that she always had been.

EPILOGUE

Shortly after they were married, Tony and Heather made an unannounced visit to Annie to deliver the letter that Grandpa Charley had left for her in Iron Post Corner. They walked up the front porch stairs and knocked on the door but there was no answer. Tony told Heather that he would check around back. As he walked around the house, he saw an older woman sitting on the back patio holding a glass of raspberry lemonade.

"Excuse me, ma'am."

The woman got up out of her chair and started toward the side of the house. When she saw Tony, she dropped her glass, which shattered on the concrete patio, covered her face with both hands and exclaimed, "Charley!"

For a split second she felt as though she had been transported back in time and she was young again. But this time Tony had come back for her.

"You are the spitting image of Charley at that age."

Tony was flattered. Heather and Tony sat and talked with Annie for hours. Before they left, they gave her the sealed envelope that Grandpa Charley had left for her, but she wasn't ready to open it yet. There was something she needed to do first.

Annie called her daughter, Lora, and asked her to come over. Annie told her that she had something to tell her that she should have shared with her long ago. Lora arrived later that evening and they sat down together at the dining room table.

"Lora, I'm sorry I've waited this long but I have something important to tell you. I need to tell you where you've really come from."

"It's OK, mom. I have known since I was 17 when I found my birth certificate with Charley's name on it. At first I had a difficult time with it but as time went on, I learned more about him and how you felt about each other through his letters to you."

Annie was shocked. She had no idea that Lora had known about Charley for all those years. Tears ran down her face.

"How did you read his letters? I always kept them locked up in the coffer chest."

"The first time Charley visited, you left the coffer chest unlocked at Grandma's house while you were outside on the porch talking to him. That's why I was unknowingly staring at him. I couldn't believe that I was looking at my father. I guess I never expected to meet him in person. When I went back in the house, I read the poem he wrote you and then I read the letters. That's when I really came to understand that you were once in love with another man and that, for whatever reason, things didn't work out because of something he had done. Were you ever able to forgive him for that?"

"We were very much in love but life never asked us what we wanted. I suppose I have always loved him and always will. However, my biggest regret is that you never knew him. He was the most amazing man I ever knew."

"Mom, tell me about my father."

"His name was Tony Charles Arthur Crambrink…"

After their conversation, Annie opened the letter that Charley had left for her and began reading:

"My dearest Annie,

Every night, in the darkness, when I close my eyes, I still see you and ask myself:

What Happens Next

My whole life all I wanted was to matter, so

I joined the Army in search of something bigger;

I was promoted again and again,

Until they put me in charge of a platoon of men;

270

At that point, I thought I had it all,

Until I met you and head over heels began to fall;

Annie, I love you still and always will;

What happens next, I can't wait to see,

As long as in the end, it's always you and me."

Her age and experience now caused her to look at the poem differently than she had all those years ago. The older Annie got, the more she understood that there was so much she didn't know. Yet she had faith that there was life after death and the sincere desire of her heart was that a reunion awaited her and Charley.

Annie walked out on the porch, closing her eyes and smelling the sea breeze and whispered, "Charley, my love, as I look up at the stars at night, may we continue communicating through our thoughts, dreams and hearts until at last we are reunited. Tell me, my love, what happens next?"

ABOUT THE AUTHOR

Clayton Lucas is a sixth generation native of Oklahoma, where he currently lives and is serving as a City Manager. He has served in municipal government for more than 17 years, including as a police officer, firefighter and urban planner. Before earning a Bachelor's degree in Geography from Fresno State University and a Master's degree in Public Administration from Pennsylvania State University, Clayton lived in Venezuela for two years where he worked to serve others, learned to love the culture and people, and became fluent in Spanish.

Clayton and his wife, Lora, have five children, Clayton III, Jonah, Willie, Henry and Heather, two of which have Type 1 Diabetes. As a result, Clayton and Lora are advocates and supporters of the Juvenile Diabetes Research Foundation (JDRF) and any organization that furthers the efforts to find a cure for Type 1 Diabetes. Clayton and his family love to travel internationally, participate in outdoor activities and spend time with family and friends. Iron Post Corner is Clayton's debut novel.

Book Club Questions

Why do you think The Lady, or the Tiger by Frank Stockton was Heather's favorite story?

Have you ever written an ending to Frank Stockton's classic tale? If so, how did Heather's ending differ from your own?

How was Heather's ending to The Lady, or the Tiger reflective of who she is and her core beliefs about life?

Is it possible for something so small and insignificant, like the sweet fragrance of honeysuckle, to awaken the past or completely alter one's perception?

There is a woman who Hank, Tony's dad, married after divorcing Ellen. Why is her name never mentioned throughout the entire story?

What kind of man was Grandpa Charley?

Why is Patty, Tony's grandmother, so tolerant of Cindy but not of Heather? Why does it matter that Heather isn't a blood relative? Should it matter?

Julie, Grandpa Charley's nurse, clearly violated hospital regulations by allowing someone into his room that she knew wasn't family. Should she have done that? Why or why not?

Why would Grandpa Charley encourage Tony to take the job with Halliburton, which would take him to another country, rather than encouraging him to move closer to home so they could spend time together? Was that the right decision?

Is it odd that Heather visited Grandpa Charley's grave so often after his death and spoke to him as if he were there? Why or why not?

Despite Grandpa Charley's last chance effort to have Heather stay in Sallisaw to wait for Tony to come back, Heather refused and decided to move on with her life by taking the job at LSU and moving back to Baton Rouge. While things eventually worked out just like Grandpa Charley wanted, do you agree with her decision? Why or why not? Was it fair for Grandpa Charley to ask that of her?

As Heather drove away from the cemetery after reading Grandpa Charley's letter, she was angry and upset as a song by Adele came on the radio. For you Adele fans, which song do you think it was?

If Tony's first reaction upon learning of his grandfather's death was to ask himself why he did not return sooner, why did he immediately decide not to return? What changed his mind?

Similarly, why had Heather never been back to visit her family's plantation home in Baton Rouge or, perhaps more importantly, her daddy's grave, especially now that she was an adult?

Why was Mr. Wight willing to let Heather out of her contract, especially since school was beginning soon, which would put him in a bind to find another teacher on such short notice?

When Heather and Tony were reunited at the cemetery, why do you think she waited so long before telling him who she was?

From the description of the coffer chest, where do you think it came from?

What do you think of Patty's motives for dating Charley, specifically to get out of Tulare and escape the life of a field laborer, keeping in mind that she was no different from any other young woman working in the fields of Central California at that time? Was she justified?

Why do you think that Annie and Charley were so enamored with each other from that first meeting at her home?

What kind of person was Annie? Did she change as she got older?

Why was Leno willing to go to such lengths to keep Charley and Annie from being together?

What did you think of Charley's idea to make paper boats at the beach?

When Charley flew back to California after learning that Annie was pregnant, why didn't he just confront her rather than just walking away?

After what happened, did Annie and Charley make the right decision to limit their contact and never mention each other to anyone? Why or why not?

At what point did you figure out what Grandpa Charley had left for Heather and Tony?

What was Heather's role within the Crambrink family? Do you think it was a mere coincidence that she found her way there as a child suffering from the death of her father or was it part of a larger plan? Did she hurt or heal the Crambrink family? Can you relate to her? Why or why not?

CPSIA information can be obtained
at www.ICGtesting.com
Printed in the USA
BVOW10s1956231117

501082BV00021B/446/P